D1226224

Text copyright © 2019 by A.G. Henley

Cover Designed by Najla Qamber Designs (www.najlaqamberdesigns.com)

Visit me at aghenley.com

Summary: A woman hires a head wrangler to try to save her ranch, but they don't get along, doggie.

CONTENTS

THE DOWNSIDE OF DACHSHUNDS

A Love & Pets Romantic Comedy, Book 3

A.G. HENLEY

Hey, readers!

Get the FREE prequel ebook to the Love & Pets series, *Love, Pugs, and Other Problems,* an exclusive short story that tells how Amelia gets Doug the pug instead of a ring! Go to aghenley.com/free-books!

Chapter One

Isabel

Dust swirls in a shaft of sunlight as I sweep the barn floor, trying to make the building presentable. I know how that sounds. It's a barn; it's supposed to be messy. But I can't help thinking that if the place is clean and orderly, maybe Tobias Coleman will take the job.

As I work, a few trail horses hang their heads over the stable walls, eyeing me while chewing mouthfuls of hay. When I finally clear the walkway, I look around with pride. The barn has never been this tidy before.

Stalls line either side of the walkway under the hayloft, and a good-sized tack room corrals the western saddles, helmets, and bridles used by guests of our dude ranch. Water buckets, barrels of feed, and piles of clean sawdust fill the area not taken up by horses, stables, and tack. The exterior of the two-story barn is painted a rich brown and bright white.

I pat my face with the candy-apple red bandanna tied around my neck. It's a warm August afternoon in the Colorado foothills. My phone camera tells me my mascara hasn't run and my thick black braid is mostly intact. My jeans are soil and sawdust free, and a swift glance at my pits allays my fear that sweat stains flood the folds of my denim shirt. Dust dims my ropers, but after Addie and I took over the ranch last year, I learned that clean boots were looked on with suspicion in these parts.

I glance at the time. Addie promised she'd be early so we can present a professional appearance. While I wait for her and Tobias, I stroke a few of the long, velvety faces that dangle over the stall doors. Apple nibbles a sugar cube from my palm and nickers in thanks. In the stall next to her, Parker's ears shoot forward.

I pause to listen. With a howl, the ranch's tomcat Rocky streaks across the barn floor and up Parker's stall door, making him rear. Following the cat, our trio of dachshunds Zip, Zap, and Zoom charge into the barn, trailing their leashes and barking uproariously. I jump back. They're covered in dark patches of what looks suspiciously like horse manure.

Rocky makes it to the hayloft where he hisses at the berserker dogs. They have no hope of catching him, but they're clearly determined to pretend they can. They jump up and down against Parker and Apple's stall doors on their stubby back legs. The horses shift back in their spaces, braying and banging against the walls.

Addie arrives last, panting and red-faced. My friend and co-owner is a wreck. Strands of her sweaty blonde hair stick to her face, one button of her matching denim shirt is undone leaving a gap where the bottom of her bra peeks out, and a dark smudge mars her cheek, which is alarming given what her dogs have apparently rolled in.

How did this farmer-in-the-dell-hell break loose in less than thirty seconds?

Jumping into action, I wave the broom to encourage Rocky to slink farther into the shadowy hayloft where the dogs can't see him. Then, I direct the bristles at the Zs to break their single-minded focus on the cat.

"Get the treat bucket!" I yell to Addie.

She runs to the tack room, and I hear her shake the plastic container. "Zs, treat time."

After a final satisfied glance at the loft, the dogs jog jauntily over to her, ears flapping. That's when I get a good whiff of them.

Ugh. I pinch my nose together with the edge of my bandana as Addie feeds them treats. We're totally rewarding bad behavior, but it gets them to focus.

"What happened?" I ask her.

My friend raises her hands, her expression bewildered. "I cut across the meadow from the cabins to make sure I got here on time. Rocky was asleep on a hay bale until the Zs caught wind of him. They pulled their leashes out of my hand and chased him, slipping and sliding in the poop—"

"Manure," I remind her. We're trying to use the right ranching words as much as possible.

She rolls her eyes. "Isa, if it looks like poop, smells like poop, and—" She makes a face, yanks a towel off the wall normally used for wiping down the saddles, and cleans her left hand, which I realize is covered in filth. "*Feels* like poop, it's poop. I'm just saying."

"What happened to you, though?" I ask.

"I chased after them," she gestures at the dogs, who pant happily now, "slipped, and my hand dove right into a huge poop nugget."

She examines her fingers, her face twisting with disgust. I carefully take the towel from her and wipe the smudge off her face.

"I'm sorry," she says. "I know we need to make a good impression."

I sigh. "At least he isn't here yet."

I spoke too soon. The Zs, lolling at our feet, suddenly rocket toward the barn door. A man stands in the entrance, arms up like he's being robbed, while the dogs race around his boots, barking. They won't bite, although they definitely give the impression that they might.

Addie and I try to call them off, but they've completely lost their heads. We chase them around like chickens. Addie grabs the leash of the smooth black and tan female, Zip, and I get the lead of the red male, Zoom. But Zap, the hairy chocolate and tan male, evades every effort to reach him. Desperate, I scoop up Zoom, Zap runs to his brother, and I snatch him up, too.

Breathing hard, I glance down. Manure—okay, fine, poop—covers the front of my shirt and tops of my thighs, and I smell like the ranch's septic tank took me for a spin and spat me out. Addie's even worse.

I wrestle my disgusted expression into a smile and turn to the newcomer.

"Tobias?" I ask with as much dignity as I can muster. "Welcome to Lazy Dog Ranch."

Chapter Two

Tobias

I stand, hands over my head, while a trio of dung-covered dachshunds race around my feet barking their fool heads off. What are weenies like these even doing on a dude ranch?

I wait for the two women to call the dogs off, which they try to do but it doesn't work, and I have a quiet laugh to myself as they chase them around the barn.

I'd help, but I don't trust dachshunds. Growing up, my aunt had one named Killer. The slack-eared son of a sausage tried to bite me every chance it got. I still have scars.

One of the women is blonde and petite, with blue eyes and a smile on her face despite being covered in crap. But it's the dark one that draws my eye. She's taller and curvier, with thick black hair and skin like buttery soft leather. Even crouched down with muck on her shirt and a stinking dog under each arm, there's something regal about her. Which is saying something.

When they finally get control of the dogs, the dark one lifts her chin and welcomes me to the ranch. Robes, crowns, and thrones come to mind again.

"I'm Isabel Costa," she says, "and this is my co-owner, Adelaide Miller."

"You can call us Isa and Addie." The blonde sticks her hand out, realizes it's covered in poo, and slowly pulls it back.

I take off my hat. "*You're* the new owners?"

My voice is heavy with skepticism, but I can't help it. Instead of horses, these women should ride BMWs; instead of dirt under their nails, they have manicures; and instead of sensible working dogs, like Australian shepherds or border collies, they have dachshunds.

Addie droops as if I yelled at her, and Isa's mouth thins dangerously.

I've obviously already put my foot in it. So to speak.

Nice work, Tobias. I need this job, and the first thing I do is question my new potential managers.

Great start.

Chapter Three

Isabel

After asking if we're really the new owners, as if it couldn't be possible, Tobias takes a long, critical look around the barn. His gaze starts at the horses, skims across the various pieces of equipment, the walls, rafters, and finally settles on Addie and me again. He doesn't smile.

Now that the wrangler's not silhouetted in the daylight behind him, I can see his face. He has bright blond hair, too light for a grown man, blue eyes, and an annoyingly reproachful expression.

What. A. Jerk.

My body tenses and my teeth grit. This isn't the first time Addie and I have gotten this reaction, especially from the mountain men who think they're the only ones who can reasonably operate a dude ranch.

"Yes, we are," I say with as much pride as I can muster while holding wriggly, poop-painted doxies. "Addie and I have owned the Lazy Dog for about eighteen months."

"And we love it," my friend says. "Maybe we haven't been here long, but it's such a special place for us." Her eyes sparkle, which makes my heart ache. Addie's become so attached to the ranch, even more than I have.

Tobias looks from me to her to the dogs, and his frown deepens. "And you're looking for a new head wrangler."

"Yes." I reposition Zap and Zoom, who are still woofing at Tobias. Zoom's long, thick hair feels sticky and foul. "Our previous head wrangler moved back to Texas a week ago to take care of his mother. We're looking to hire someone as soon as possible."

He also left because he thought we were a couple of idiots with lady parts, but you won't catch me telling any applicants that. Anyway, I don't need to. Tobias already seems to share the same opinion.

His eyes take in the barn again, and he nods. "I'd expect so."

I have a hard time not openly glaring at the man. We have a small operation compared to many other dude ranches in Colorado, but our property is gorgeous, our herd of thirty horses are healthy and, for the most part, happy. The barn, arena, and paddock are well maintained. What does he see that's so disappointing—other than Addie and me?

"Please have a look around," I say. "We'll go outside and clean up so we can speak properly."

Addie and I hurry out to the hose and put the Zs down, keeping our boot heels on their leashes as we wash our hands and the leashes. Nothing we can do about our clothes unless we want to interview Tobias soaking wet.

The dogs' baths will have to wait. Their ears wiggle and their long bellies skim the tall grass as they sniff around. I sigh. When they aren't defending the world from feline marauders and rolling in feces, they're very sweet. But on days like this, I secretly wonder if dachshunds really belong on a ranch.

"He seems pretty serious," Addie whispers.

"Judgmental," I say.

She blinks, her blue eyes wide. "What makes you say that?"

I glance toward the barn door and lower my voice even more. "Didn't you see his expression? He looked like a restaurant inspector who caught us rubbing *E. coli* on the kitchen counters."

"Well, we are covered in poop, Isa, and the Zs weren't exactly welcoming."

"He still doesn't need to look down on us."

She elbows me. "Does the fact that he's good-looking cut him any slack?"

I sniff and instantly regret it. "I didn't notice."

"Sure you didn't. I've known you since we were eighteen; you don't miss anything. We may have bad luck with men, you and me, but we can spot the cute ones."

I roll my eyes. "Come on, let's get back inside. He's probably examining the horses for signs of abuse and neglect."

Addie snorts. "Now who's being judgmental?"

I lead the way, Zap's lead firmly in hand. Addie has the other two. The dogs trot ahead, tails wagging, cats and dangerous strangers forgotten.

As I expected, Tobias is inside a stall examining the teeth of Jughead, one of our quarter horses. I glance at Addie with an eyebrow raised. She shoots me a warning look, but ice still frosts my words when I speak.

"Our herd is in excellent condition. Dr. Garner was just out last week and gave them a clean bill of health."

To the tune of several thousand dollars. I'd had to move money around to cover the expense. Tobias makes a non-committal sound, which worries me.

The guests of Lazy Dog Ranch come to *ride, reconnect, and relax*. That's our slogan, in fact. It features prominently on our website and all our marketing materials. A healthy herd is a key to our success.

Garner must have raised his rates once we bought the ranch because what he charged was notably more than Tom and Betty Richardson, who sold Addie and me the ranch at a nice discount, told us they paid for regular veterinary exams. At least our canine veterinarian, Dr. Travis Brewer, charges reasonable amounts to see the Zs.

Tobias runs his hand along Jughead's haunch. "Tell me about the position."

I know from Tobias' application that he last worked as the head wrangler of a dude ranch in Wyoming, but I give him a rundown of the responsibilities anyway.

Oversee the care and training of the herd, manage and maintain the barn, the arena, the paddock, and the other wranglers, of which there are currently two. Lead trail rides when needed. Additional duties as assigned, like socializing with the guests once or twice a week at different evening events. Keep Addie and me apprised of any problems with the above.

"All personnel decisions are ours, and we will set the budget," I say.

"Of course, we'll take your input into serious consideration when making decisions," Addie adds.

I smile thinly. "Of course. Now, tell us about your experience, Tobias."

He squats, back to us, and lifts Jughead's hoof to see the underside. "I grew up on my parents' small cattle ranch outside Estes Park. I've worked with horses all my life."

Addie and I nod like bobbleheads on a desk. Estes Park is about half an hour's drive north from here.

"So you left Wyoming because you wanted to be near your family?" Addie asks.

He laughs, short and hard. "Not exactly."

I wait, but he doesn't say anything else. "Why did you leave your last position?"

"I missed home."

He flashes a smile, and I'm temporarily blinded. It's wide and white, and it crinkles his eyes in a way that makes him look even younger than his early-thirties, which I estimate to be his age.

"You don't exactly want to be near family, but you missed home?" Addie sounds puzzled.

"That's about right." Tobias moves expertly from hoof to hoof, checking all four.

I frown again and cross my arms before remembering that I have half-dried manure on my shirt. How I forgot with the smell, I can't say.

He glances at us and tilts his head, seeming to give in. "Family responsibilities brought me back to Colorado."

I nod, satisfied for now. I'll check his references either way. "We have accommodations for you on the ranch, a small apartment near the other staff housing for reasonable rent. Board is included," I say.

"I won't need it."

"The hours are long, as I'm sure you know. Are you positive you don't want to stay on property?" I ask.

"No thanks. But don't worry. I stay until the job gets done. Always."

I suddenly picture him riding alone with snow-capped mountains in the distance; the tragic star of a modern western . . . although I have no idea what makes him tragic. Maybe it's the wariness in his eyes that sets my intuition to tingling. He's been hurt.

Addie and I follow him as he makes his way into Apple's stall. His examination of her is quicker.

"The other wranglers, Amanda and Wayne, are very good," Addie says. "They're out leading rides, but if you stick around, you can meet them."

We hire local staff as much as possible, and we supplement with college kids during the summer high season for our wait staff, housekeepers, and childcare workers, which we call kid wranglers. Except for a few weeks around the winter holidays, turning a profit was much more challenging during the snowy months and the shoulder seasons of spring and fall.

Tobias reads my mind. "How's your occupancy?"

He went right for the jugular, didn't he? I swallow and avoid Addie's eyes.

"We're staying full," she says. Barely, I add to myself.

The truth is, we're having a hard time staying afloat, and the generous salary we're offering for a head wrangler will cut sharply into our bottom line. But without one, we can't keep our herd strong and our guests happy. Without the horses, we have an okay hotel with nice views in the Colorado foothills.

The bottom line? We need Tobias Coleman a lot more than he probably needs us.

"I've sent you the salary and benefits already, and you've seen the ranch. I'm sure you have questions but are you interested in the position?" I ask.

He studies us. Not in the appreciative or leering way a man sometimes looks at women, but in the way he was just examining our horses. As if our outward appearances can tell him the soundness of our business plan, the health of our bank account, and the strength of our entrepreneurial acumen.

"I do have a question," he says. "How did you two city girls end up here?"

His tone is curious, not demeaning, but I grit my teeth at the word *girls*. Addie and I are successful, capable businesswomen, which he'll find out soon enough—if he takes the job.

Probably sensing my annoyance, Addie responds. "Isa and I have been best friends since college. We both worked in tech sales at the same company in Denver after we graduated college. We were good at our jobs, but we couldn't stand the idea of traveling constantly for work, spending our days in soulless cubicles when we weren't traveling, and attending endless meetings for the next three decades. So about two years ago, we hatched a BHAG over a few drinks at our favorite bar and . . . here we are."

He squints at us before moving on to Parker's stall. "A BHAG?"

I jump in. "A Big Hairy Audacious Goal. Have you ever had one?"

Tobias greets the Appaloosa and runs a hand over his spotted, brown and white hide. "Can't say I have. Yours was to own a dude ranch?"

"It was to own and build *something*," Addie answers. "We wanted to work for ourselves, stay in one place, be outdoors more, and grow something that didn't revolve around money and screens. We made a list of things that sounded interesting, pooled our savings, and waited for an opportunity. My parents and I visited this ranch ten years ago or so when the Richardsons owned it, and we'd stayed in touch. I heard they were looking to retire and were selling at a fair price and . . . here we are."

Addie and I glance at each other. Buying and operating a dude ranch sounded so romantic at the time. Riding horses, entertaining our guests, enjoying gorgeous sunrises and sunsets in the Rocky Mountains. What wasn't to love?

Now, we don't have to travel, there isn't a cubicle in sight, and our lives revolve around anything but technology. But as for building and growing . . . we wish.

"One more question, then," he says. "What's with the dogs?"

"The Zs?" Addie says. "They're mine, but Isa knows them as well as I do. We thought they'd love ranch life, and we were right about that." She points to each one, introducing them as they sniff around the outside of the stalls.

Zap lifts his leg on Jughead's door, the pee puddling before soaking into the dirt floor, and Tobias shakes his head.

"Dogs like that should be in apartments or on back porches. Not on a ranch. They'll only cause trouble."

Addie's eyes grow wide. Mine narrow.

"Thanks for your advice, but if you accept the position, you should know that these dogs come with the ranch. Just like Addie and me." I let that sink in with the pee. "So, now you know all about us, Tobias. And you know about the job. Do you want to work with us or not?"

Please, please, please say yes. Like him or not, we're out of applicants. And no matter how negative he might be, Tobias' experience makes him perfect for the job.

My hands grow clammy as I wait for him to answer. Addie worries the inside of her lip with her teeth, something she tends to do when she's anxious. Tobias pats Parker on the rump before exiting the stall.

"I'll let you know. It was good to meet you both."

He shakes our hands, sets his hat back on his head, and walks out of the barn, leaving me wondering exactly who was interviewing who.

Chapter Four

❧

Tobias

I think about the job as I drive my truck back to my parents' place. I'd be an idiot to take it. The owners are clueless, the dogs are ridiculous, and my guess is the ranch will fold within a year.

I've worked on dude ranches long enough to know a full house when I see one, and Lazy Dog is far from full. August should be their best month, the month that helps them survive the lean winters in the mountains when herds still had to be fed, trained, and cared for and staff still required salaries. I don't know how Isa and Addie lasted through the first winter, much less how they'll make it through a second.

But . . . there's something about the women that makes me want to help. Maybe it's Addie's obvious love for the place or Isa's pride. She won't go down without a fight, that one. Maybe it's that if the ranch is sold, it could be bought by some prick that hands it over to a nameless and faceless hotel chain, or worse, a residential developer.

Or maybe I just need the paycheck. Tyler's meds aren't cheap.

I run through the grocery list in my head. I'll stop at the store on the way home, and get Ty ice cream for after dinner. Poor kid's been stuck at home all day, probably bored out of his skull. School doesn't start for a few more weeks.

I call my mom on my cellphone. Tyler picks up, his voice weak. My hands tighten on the wheel. "What's up buddy? Are you okay?"

"Yeah, . . . I just ran to get the phone."

I relax a little. "I'm headed to the grocery store. Can you ask Grandma if she needs anything?"

He yells into the receiver. "Grandmadoweneedanythin-gatthestore?"

Or at least, that's what it sounds like as I hold my phone away from my ringing ear. I wait for an answer, which comes a second later.

"She wants flowers."

"Flowers?"

"For baking bread."

"Oh, flour. Got it. Anything else?"

"And she wants Snickers bars, Warheads, and Twizzlers, but the bites instead of the ropes."

I smile. "She does, does she? Grandma has a sweet tooth today."

"Yeeeeep." He draws out the word, and then he coughs. The sound, thick and choked, makes me cringe every single time I hear it.

"Did you use your nebulizer this afternoon?"

"Yeah, but it didn't work so good. My lungs have been sticky all day."

Sticky is my seven-year-old son's word for clogged. It's as good a description as any for what happens in the lungs of someone with cystic fibrosis. I wish I didn't know half of what I do about that frigging disease.

"Maybe Grandma can give you your thinner?" Mucus thinners help him clear his lungs a little and breathe easier.

"She did. I'll be okay, Dad. I've gotta go."

"What are you doing?" I already know. It's about all he can do when he's sticky.

"I'm building a massive roller coaster in Minecraft. It's really cool."

"I want to see it when I get home, all right? Love you, partner."

"Love you, too, Dad." He hangs up.

My heart breaks a little every time I hear the absence of his voice. Most parents only worry about not seeing their kids as much once they're off to college or new jobs or whatever. With the mortality rates of CF, once Tyler reaches that age, I'll have to worry about never seeing him again. The life expectancy is better than it used to be, but I could easily outlive my son.

I shake off the dark thoughts as I drive into the small mountain town of Estes Park and head for the Safeway. Estes is the gateway to beautiful Rocky Mountain National Park, where bear, elk, and moose roam alongside plenty of tourists.

I park at the grocery store and say hello to an old friend of my dad's on the way in. As I pick through the apples, I think again about if I want to answer to two women who have no idea how to manage a herd or run a guest ranch.

I have nothing against female bosses. Really. But I'm not good at taking orders from people who don't know what they're doing.

On the other hand, Tyler has no shortage of medical appointments with his pulmonologist, respiratory therapist, and other specialists, and those bills aren't cheap. We need good health care, and this job supposedly offers it.

I debate with myself all the way through the cereal and rice aisles and into the baking section, but as I reach for a powdery sack of flour, Isabel's flashing dark eyes come to mind. I suppose

I could live with a little incompetence to see those eyes—and those curves—at work every day.

We might disagree. We might even fight. I might quit or she might fire me.

But it might be worth it.

Chapter Five

Isabel

I knock on the door of the Crested Butte guest cabin, one of ten on the ranch, and look out over the Lazy Dog as I wait for an answer.

Our cabins are named for various mountain towns around the state like Telluride, Durango, and Grand Lake. This one sits in the middle of the long and narrow ranch. The stables, arena, and paddock are to the east and the activity center and combination dining room and lodge are west, nearer to the ranch's entrance. The owner's house, which Addie and I share, is uphill from here, overlooking the property.

My breath catches as I gaze at our BHAG. The Colorado sky overhead is as blue as a dyed Easter egg. The peaks surrounding the ranch are built to stun. Cheerful Breezy Creek burbles along in front of me, traveling the length of the ranch, and a few of our herd can be seen off in the distance, enjoying a day off in the pasture. In other words, it's heaven.

If only more people knew that.

I sigh and enter the cabin to check the housekeepers' work. New guests will arrive in the morning.

The cabin is typical of the others in that it has a small living area with a gas fireplace, a bedroom or two, a bathroom, and it's decorated in a modern rustic style. Some of our initial capital went into freshening the rooms and updating the sagging bathrooms.

I stop in the entryway when I hear singing. And not just any music—disco. *Not again.*

I brace myself as a balding black man wearing only tube socks and a towel around his pot belly struts out of the bathroom singing into an empty toilet paper roll. It's *Le Freak* this time.

Cliff, our head housekeeper, shimmies over to me, singing and bouncing his hips to the groove. When he gives me his best seductive look, it's hard not to laugh. He's fifteen years my senior, although good genes help him hide it, and he sells his performance.

"Freak out!" He sings as the song finishes.

"Cliff, we've talked about this."

He pulls an AirPod out of one ear and pouts. "I know, but when *Le Freak* comes on, I just have to dance."

I throw up my hands. "But why without clothes? What if the guests had come back? What if the next guests had arrived early?"

"Then they, too, would get an eyeful of this Beast of Boogie." He spins and shakes his butt at me again for good measure.

I shake my head, frustrated but amused. "Are you done in here?"

"Done like a ski run," he rhymes.

"You were supposed to be off an hour ago," I chide.

He tears off the towel with a flourish. I'm tempted to close my eyes, just in case, but he has his khaki work shorts under it as always. He snatches the company-issued dark green polo shirt with the Lazy Dog Ranch logo off the bed and pulls it over his head.

"The guests left two hours late," he says. "Dale is out sick today, and I let Marisol and Kristie go home instead of having to wait to clean the room."

And therein lies a big reason I won't let my eccentric head housekeeper go. First, he never dances naked in front of guests. Second, third, and fourth, he gets the job done, he does it well, and . . . he's willing to work for what we can pay him. As a bonus, he's a local who's been at the ranch for ten years. That kind of loyalty can't be bought. Even if he is *un freak*.

I pat his shoulder, fatigue spreading through me. "Thank you for staying."

I walk through the cabin checking the beds, fingering the flat surfaces for dust, and inspecting the bathtub and shower. Spotless. Not even a stray hair. Cliff lounges against the wall, still humming the song under his breath. "All to your satisfaction?"

I have to admit it is. "But *please* try not to do this again. One of these days it will be a guest instead of Addie or me."

"Duly noted. Have a good evening, Isabel." He accentuates my name and sweeps past me, pushing his cleaning cart out the door in front of him.

"Hey, Cliff," I hear Addie say. "Have you seen Isa?"

"You'll find your partner in crime inside, still stunned by my virtuosity."

"Okay, thanks." My friend hurries in, her face flushed. She grabs my hands and jumps up and down. "You won't believe who's coming!"

"Who?" I hesitate to get excited. We've had so many ups and downs this year—and mostly downs—that it's hard to muster the enthusiasm.

"Kate Jordan," she says.

I blink. "Really?"

"Yes!" Addie looks like a balloon ready to pop. When she gets excited, her face goes very red. "Her assistant, Axel Weber, called to make the reservation. He wanted to let me know that she has some dietary restrictions, room requirements, she's allergic to bee stings—"

"Does she carry an EpiPen?"

"Who knows? Who cares? It's Kate Jordan!" Addie sighs when she catches my evil eye. "I'll check the first aid supplies and make sure we have some, okay? Now, will you be excited?"

"And check that they aren't expired," I say, but anticipation and anxiety do tickle my gut. Kate is a hugely popular film star who probably has millions of followers on social media. If she raves to them about her visit to Lazy Dog Ranch . . .

"Wow. Kate Jordan," I say.

"I know! Isn't it amazing?" She hugs me. "Have you heard from Tobias?"

"Not yet."

I hate that so much of our future relies on whether stern Tobias Coleman takes the wrangler job. I haven't heard from him since his interview two days ago, although I emailed him with an official offer yesterday. I keep checking my phone, hoping to see a positive response. And now, with Kate Jordan on the way, it's more important than ever to hire someone, anyone, to take charge of the barn.

I tug out my phone again, check my email, and squeal. "He wants the job!"

Addie hoots. "We have to get ready! Which cabin should we put Kate in? She needs two, one for her and one for a guest she's bringing. Maybe Durango and Breckenridge? I need to talk to Wanda about the meals, too. Kate's a strict vegan and . . ."

"Wait, when is she getting here?"

"Two weeks!"

I laugh. "Addie, we have plenty of time to plan—"

Too late, she's on a roll. As she goes on about everything we need to do, I fantasize about what this could mean. Tobias is taking the job; one challenge met. Now, if Kate loves her visit, it could change the course of our business and be the break that we desperately need.

But break is a funny word. You can *catch a break* or something can *make or break* your dreams.

Kate Jordan, A-list actress, will no doubt be one or the other for us.

Chapter Six

Tobias

"Good luck on your first day, Dad," Tyler says.

He's sitting at the table in Mom's eat-in kitchen, watching a cartoon show about robots and demolishing homemade waffles with maple syrup. His curly blond head looks like someone vacuumed it straight up. How do pillows manage that all on their own? I ruffle his wild hair more and kiss his forehead. He coughs.

"No riding with Grandpa today, okay?" I say.

He nods, but his mouth turns down. I glance at my mother, who has a worried eye on her Ty as she loads the dishwasher.

The day after my interview at Lazy Dog, I'd had some errands to run, including getting Tyler registered at the local elementary school. Ty had had a good morning, Mom told me, so Dad had let him ride with him while he'd checked some fencing. But Tyler came back wheezing, coughing, and running a slight fever. He'd had to rest the remainder of the afternoon. I'd been so worried about him, I didn't respond to Isa's emailed job offer.

I finally accepted it yesterday. I'd made more at my last ranch in Wyoming. But the benefits here included quality health care coverage for Tyler and me.

So—I'm the newest employee of the Lazy Dog Ranch.

Normally, I'll get to work before dawn to help with corralling the horses and getting them ready for the day, but Isa asked me to come a bit later for a quick orientation. She also said something about an important guest coming soon.

I give my mom a hug and kiss her graying head. She used to have blonde hair, but after Tyler was born, and Ellen, my wife, took off, Mom had gone gray. I have a few grays myself now, too.

She cups my face. "Good luck, Toby."

I smile. She's the only person in the world who calls me Toby instead of Tobias. No one except her seems to think the nickname fits me.

"Thanks, Mom. I should be back for dinner."

I drive the half-hour to Lazy Dog, thinking about what might lie ahead. I expect to find half-trained wranglers, whiny guests, and a barely functional barn. Don't get me started on the management. At least the herd seems to be in good shape.

I pull into the employee parking lot. I'm supposed to meet Isa in the business office, which is in the main lodge. I glance at myself in the window of the truck before I go.

I'm wearing jeans, a simple western shirt, boots, and a cowboy hat. I own chaps and spurs, although I only use them when training horses. Still, I've learned that guests and owners alike expect you to look the part of a cowboy.

My tired expression in the glass can't be helped; Tyler had a rough night.

I'm a little early, so I stroll in, taking my time to look around. The lodge is a two-story wood building with scores of windows facing the mountains to the south. The creek runs north of the lodge, which gives the lodge nice views from either side.

Inside, the place is decorated in what I call want-to-be western, as if it can't decide whether to be modern or rustic. It's not my favorite, but it's popular right now from the websites I visited in my job search.

A small lobby facing the parking lot holds a check-in and concierge desk. I introduce myself to the woman and head into the dining room beyond to wait for Isa. A few guests are there, enjoying their mugs of coffee and breakfast.

I sit by the window to savor the peace and quiet for a minute, but a scream from the kitchen, followed by a stream of cussing, cuts it short. The guests startle and look that way. I rush into the kitchen to see if I can help.

A small brown-haired woman, about twenty, is on fire.

Not her body, yet, but her apron is smoking, and she's understandably howling like she's crossing hell's doorstep. A heavyset woman with tight gray curls aims a commercial fire extinguisher at the girl.

"Close your eyes and hold your breath, Myra!" The older woman yells.

She lets fly, and Myra shrieks as the stream of pale yellow powder hits her chest and explodes up into her face. When the stream runs out, Myra looks like a giant flower pollinated on her.

Behind her, a pot of something oily has overflowed onto the burner, which must have sparked. And it's still on fire.

"Grab the other extinguisher," the older woman shouts to me, pointing at the wall. I yank the device out of its cradle, step around Myra, and aim the spray at the range. A stream of soapy foam hits the burner and the pot, putting out the flames but instantly ruining whatever's in there.

The door to the kitchen swings open, and Isa and Addie run in. Their eyes go wide when they see Myra covered in yellow dust and the foamy stew swamping the range.

Addie takes the crying, red-faced girl's hand. "Myra, are you hurt?"

She shakes her head and forces out some words. "N-n-n no. I-I'm okay. Just scared."

Isa's eyes are hard as she looks over the range, but she softens as she speaks to the older woman. "What about you, Wanda? Are you injured?"

"No, but look at the state of my kitchen!"

Now that I hear their voices, I know the cussing came from Wanda. I move a trashcan under the range, where the oily, foamy mixture's dribbling onto the floor.

Isa turns to me. "Thank you for your help, Tobias. If you'd like to have a seat in the dining room, we'll be with you in a few minutes. I'm sorry for the delay."

Her words are polite, but the snippy way she says them tells me she's frustrated. I hang the extinguisher up and head to my table. But I can't help shaking my head as I go. Did I say they'd be out of business in a year? I give this place six months.

The guests watch as I come out, clearly wondering what was going on in the kitchen. I pull out my most reassuring, laid-back smile and raise my hands.

"Don't worry, folks, everything's fine. Great cooks can't work their magic without a few kitchen calamities. Apologies for the disruption."

A college-aged waiter gives me a funny look before refilling the diners' coffee mugs and speaking to them with a smile. He's probably wondering who the heck I am, but I don't mind. I've never been one to sit around and do nothing when there's an emergency.

A new commotion outside draws my attention. The weenie dogs are jumping up and down against the glass door and barking their fool heads off, wanting inside.

The front desk worker, who's busy with a guest, keeps throwing desperate glances at the door. Shaking my head for the second time in three minutes, I go outside. They don't come at me this time, but they keep barking.

"C'mere," I say to them. "I've got something for you." I reach into my chest pocket where I keep wrapped peppermints, treats for the horses. Hopefully, the candy will distract them long enough to get them to end their unholy noise.

I unwrap one for each of the dogs, and I'm offering them to them when Isa rushes out.

"Stop! Don't give them those. Peppermint can make them sick." Her dark eyes blaze.

I stand and pocket the candies. "Just trying to help."

"Well . . . don't." Isa pushes her hair back from her face and closes her eyes for a moment. "Come with me, please."

I swallow the angry, peppermint-flavored response that pops into my mouth. Isa marches around the corner of the building, dogs at her heels, to a sunny office at the back corner. The windows inside look out on the same majestic mountain views as the dining room. She invites me to sit.

"Exciting morning," I say.

"Not the word I'd use for it." She rubs a temple.

I hoped a touch of empathy came through but maybe not.

"Addie and I are pleased you accepted the position." She doesn't look all that pleased.

"I'm glad to be here."

"I've asked Wayne, the wrangler who's been with us the longest, to meet us here and show you, er, the ropes. I'm sorry for the late start today, but it's our checkout and check-in day, which is always busy. Oh, and by the way, we're expecting an important guest in a few weeks."

"Blake Shelton's coming?" I joke.

Her face is blank. "No. It's an actress."

So much for joking around . . . and for the musical tastes of my new manager. She clearly doesn't listen to country or even watch TV.

"I need you to fill out a little paperwork before you get started." She pushes a pile of paper across the desk to me.

I shake my head. "I don't do paperwork."

I'm teasing again, but I must not make it obvious, because she pushes back in her seat, her face pinched.

"Tobias, I know your experience is on larger ranches with larger staffs. But the Lazy Dog is a small operation. To make this place successful, we all have to pitch in and do things we prefer not to do."

I stare for a second, my jaw clenching against the floodwater of words on my tongue, but the words burst out anyway.

"In my first ten minutes here, I helped squelch a kitchen emergency and," I jerk a thumb at the dachshunds curled at her feet, "tamed three over-excited dogs that don't belong on a ranch. Now you're questioning my willingness to pitch in? Lady, I'm not sure you know how to manage a sandwich, much less a ranch."

Okay, maybe that wasn't fair, but my campfire's burning hot, as my mom says.

She leans forward, her eyes slits. "Thank you for your help this morning. But I suggest you keep your opinions to yourself if you want to keep your new job. I can manage the business of this ranch just fine."

We glare at each other for a second before someone knocks on the office door.

"Come in," Isa barks.

A guy about forty, dressed a lot like me, with tan, weathered skin and a red nose that tells me he takes the sun and booze in equal measure stands outside. Isa waves him in and introduces us in as few words as possible. Wayne's smile fades at the furious expression on her face, while I shake his hand with a grip that could choke a snake. He glances from me to Isa, who's shooting invisible darts at my head.

He nods to me cautiously. "Nice to meet you, boss. Glad you made it."

Isa's expression darkens; my guess is she's starting to regret that I made it. Time for a tactical retreat. I snatch the paperwork off her desk.

"I'll get this done on my lunch break."

I walk out of the office without another word. Wayne's about five inches shorter than me, so he has to hurry to keep up with my long strides. Just when I think I've had the last word, Isa barks something in another language that sounds a lot like an insult and slams the door behind us. Wayne scoots forward like he was shot.

Infuriating, exasperating woman.

What was I thinking taking this job?

Chapter Seven

Isabel

"Infuriating, exasperating man," I say for the third time tonight.

Addie and I sit in Adirondack chairs on the deck of our house, previously the Richardson family home, glasses of red wine in hand.

The place isn't small, but it isn't huge—three bedrooms and as many baths. I use the master bedroom, Addie has a large secondary bedroom on the main floor, and there's a guest room upstairs. It could do with some updating, but we're comfortable here, and we adore this deck.

The Zs snooze at our feet, worn out from a day of running around the ranch and chasing critters. Zip jerks in her sleep as if she's still after them. Zoom's tail wags, just at the tip, and I wonder if he's remembering some praise he got today, or if he's reliving a happy memory. Zap sleeps peacefully, something I'm guaranteed not to do after the day I had.

Addie clears her throat. "Well, I think he's—"

"A chauvinist? As pig-headed as a mule?"

Addie looks confused. "Isn't a mule mule-headed?"

"Does he really think he's above paperwork? He probably thinks it's *women's* work."

"Um, Isa? You're kind of talking to yourself at this point."

I take a deep breath and stop. "Sorry. What were you saying?"

"I think Tobias is one of those people who says what he means." She thinks about it. "He's direct."

I make a scoffing sound.

She softens her voice. "You're direct, too, Isa."

"That's different."

"How?"

"I'm his supervisor." I try to keep a straight face but fail.

My best friend laughs, a sweet sound that never fails to make my tense shoulders drop a few inches. "Remember Chris? I'm not sure you could've *been* more direct with him."

I open my mouth, but nothing sensible comes out. Chris was our director of sales at the Denver technology company we worked for before escaping cube life and moving here. He was a good guy, yet Addie was right. I never hesitated to tell him what I thought.

I huff. "Well, this is still different. Tobias clearly thinks we're unqualified morons."

"You don't know that. And anyway, weren't you saying the other day that we desperately need a good head wrangler and specifically him? What are you trying to do, chase him off?"

"I'm trying to make him understand that he works for us."

Her voice is gentle when she responds. "I'm sure he understands that very well. Listen, he knows a lot more than us about what makes a successful guest ranch, at least when it comes to the equine program. Maybe we should ask for his help instead of getting uppity with him?"

"*Uppity?*" My mouth quirks. "Is that what I'm being?"

"I mean, a little. But you know I love you anyway."

I wrap my sweater closer around me, rest my head back against the chair, and watch the stars twinkle for a few minutes.

"We're doing okay, right, Addie?" My voice is uncertain. "Like, we're not making a total mess of this, are we? We won't end up crawling back to Denver looking for jobs after losing our life savings in a BHAG gone wrong?"

Addie doesn't answer right away. "Remember what we said when we started out? We knew we'd make mistakes, but we'd learn from them and move on. Maybe this is one of those times."

I close my eyes, feeling guilty. I hate losing my temper. Tobias pushes buttons inside me that I haven't completely identified. He could be perfectly nice under all that poker-faced arrogance, but he needs to understand: this place is more than a job for Addie and me.

We lived in modest apartments for the first ten years of our careers, hoarding our commissions while our coworkers bought BMWs and first homes and traveled to places like Iceland, Indonesia, or the Virgin Islands—a misnomer if I've ever heard one based on their stories.

We didn't know exactly what we wanted to do with the money we saved, but we knew we *didn't* want to be in tech sales for the rest of our lives.

So when we had the opportunity to buy the Richardson ranch, we threw ourselves and our savings at the place. Every penny the two of us have is sunk into this place. It's exhilarating and terrifying.

"So, you think I should apologize to him?" I ask.

I did accuse him of being lazy and called him the equivalent of a horse's ass, a word I became all too familiar with growing up with my feisty Italian grandmother. Not to mention I slammed the door on him.

"Oh, you know men. He's probably over it by now," Addie says, except I hear a *but* coming. "But on the other hand, clearing the air would be the professional thing to do."

I hadn't seen Tobias after our argument today. We'd already drawn our lines. He stayed near the barn and I kept close to the business office.

"Okay. I'll talk to him." Sometime. Although I know Addie's right, I'm not in that much of a hurry.

"Good. Now that that's settled, what else do we need for Kate's visit?"

I groan. We have a few weeks, but the woman's list of preferences and needs is longer than my aunt Lucia's fingernails. My heartstrings twang painfully at the thought of my family. I've been too busy to visit all summer. I need to plan a trip to Denver to see them in a month or two when the high season ends.

My parents and brother Emilio thought Addie and I had lost our minds when I told them our plan, but they eased off once we made the move. They even came for a long weekend back in the spring.

"I've got her list. And I'll arrange for a special delivery of vegan staples and make sure we have Brandy and Teresa on call for massages and facials," I say. We don't have a spa at the Lazy Dog. Building one is in the five-year plan, but we offer spa services in-cabin when our guests ask for them.

"At least Kate's assistant, Axel, is organized," Addie says. "He's been nice and easy to work with."

"Is he coming?" I ask.

"I don't think so. But Kate's psychic and tarot card reader is."

I sit up. "Her what?"

"Her psychic and tarot card reader. Her name's Bianca."

"That's ridiculous."

"What's ridiculous about the name Bianca?" Addie grins; she knows what I mean. "Apparently, Kate doesn't travel anywhere without her."

I flop my arms out on the armrests. "What are we getting ourselves into?"

"If everything goes right, a great recommendation of the ranch and a bunch of future reservations." Addie calmly sips her wine.

Something flutters in the pine tree beside the deck, bringing me back to the present of the cool, dark night. Whatever the future brings, at least tonight we're sitting on our own deck in the mountains instead of dragging ourselves across some godforsaken airport or another after a delayed flight home from somewhere we didn't want to go in the first place.

"We can do this." I reach for my best friend's hand. "We can make Kate's stay a massive success."

"You bet we can!" Addie says. "So long as Myra doesn't burn down the kitchen, you and Tobias don't kill each other, the Zs don't get into Kate's cabin covered in poop, and Cliff isn't, well, Cliff."

I take it back. We're doomed.

Chapter Eight

Tobias

"She's a total pain in the hindquarters," I say.

"Yes, so you've told us," Mom says mildly, her head bent over a crossword puzzle game on her phone. She used to have those big books of puzzles lying around, but a year or two ago she started using electronic versions. I kind of miss the books. They remind me of the easier days of being a kid.

Tyler lies on the couch beside me. His head's in my lap and his eyes are on the Broncos' preseason game against the Falcons that Dad is watching.

"Tell us again what she called you," my son asks.

Mom sighs. "Toby, I don't like you cursing around Tyler in any language."

I smooth my son's hair away from his forehead. "One more time. Okay, partner?" I tell him the word, mimicking the way Isa said it, and he giggles.

"Oh come on, Lock, are you an NFL quarterback or not?"

My dad's decked out in his ancient Elway jersey and covered

by a fleece orange and blue blanket my sister, Tamara, gave him last Christmas. He drinks a beer out of a commemorative glass mug he bought after the Broncos were in the Super Bowl a few years ago.

"Yeah, Lock, you—" Tyler repeats the word I'd told him.

My mother throws me an exasperated look. I pat my son's hip. "That's enough, Ty. We may not know what it means, but we know it's a bad word, so it's off-limits."

Dad's still muttering about the blown pass. His thinning hair is mussed from being under a cowboy hat all day. I want to ask him how things went with moving the cattle to the new pasture today, but I know better than to try to have a conversation with him when a game's on.

"Maybe you should talk to her about how you're feeling?" Mom says.

I throw up a hand. "There's no talking to that woman. She's set herself against me for some reason."

"Well, what about your other supervisor? What did you say her name was? Adele?"

"Addie." I think about it. Isa's business partner does seem more . . . approachable. Or at least less likely to call me names to my face. It might work to ask her for advice on how to handle her not-so-better half.

"Could work," I say. "But it might take a few days to find the time. They're expecting some Hollywood actress, and everyone's focused on that."

"That sounds exciting," Mom says.

I think it sounds like a lot of extra hassle and expense for one person, but having a high-profile guest is usually a good thing for a ranch—so long as they enjoy their stay.

Dad mutters a stream of unintelligible, but definitely unhappy, comments about his Broncos. He drops a bowl of chewed-up sunflower seed shells onto a side table. "If they're going to play like this, I'm going to bed."

Mom and I don't answer. We know he won't.

I kiss the top of Tyler's head. "It's time for bed for us, too, cowboy."

He whines and snuggles down into the couch cushions. "Five more minutes?"

"It's already eight-thirty. And it's time for," I lower my voice in a mock scary voice, "the *vest*."

I hope he'll laugh as he has before when I've said it that way, but he only nods and gets up. He's pretty obedient for a second grader—the result of having had way too much on his thin shoulders all his life.

The vest is our tool for airway clearance therapy. It hooks up to a hose, powered by a generator, to gently shake Tyler's chest and loosen the mucus so he can cough it up. The treatment takes about thirty minutes twice a day. We usually read at night while he wears it, then I collapse in bed. Wrangling starts early. I stand and stretch.

Mom puts her pen down. "You go get some sleep, Toby. I can read with him."

"Thanks, but I've got it." Reading with my boy during his treatments is one thing I can do. I swing Ty over my shoulder, earning that giggle, and hang him upside down in front of my dad. "Give Grandpa a goodnight kiss."

Dad yanks his attention away from the TV long enough to kiss Tyler's forehead and then pretend to gobble him up. I swing him back upright for Grandma's kiss.

"I love you, Tyler-bug," she says.

I carry my son upstairs to his room, my old room, which is covered in his Broncos posters and my blue 4H ribbons. A trophy from winning my first rodeo when I was around his age sits on a shelf.

I want to get our own place eventually, but ranch hours are erratic and Ty can't stay by himself yet. When my job in Wyoming ended, I asked to move home and pay rent to my parents. Although I'm grateful they agreed, living with my parents is humiliating.

I'd had a hard time doing everything myself after Ellen left—working, taking care of Ty, feeding us, and keeping the house from becoming a Superfund site. I had to come home, was the truth of it. I needed help. Now Mom watches Ty during the day, makes dinner for all of us, and Dad takes him to his many medical appointments.

As I help my son into the vest and he picks a book, I try not to think about how quickly hopes and dreams become hospital beds and deadly diagnoses. Instead, I focus on how lucky I am to have the chance to lie here with my son listening to him read, lucky to have a job, lucky to have good health care now.

Losing my job at the Lazy Dog isn't an option. I need to clear the air with Isa soon and then hold my tongue.

Somehow.

Chapter Nine

Isabel

Addie and I are ready bright and early the morning of Queen Kate's arrival. I've started calling her that in my head because surely only a queen requires this much preparation.

The dogs charge out of the house before I can get the door all the way open. They're extra-animated this morning; they must sense our anticipation.

While Addie checks in with our guests at breakfast, I go to find Cliff. He's in the housekeeping office at the back of the activity center, an area of contained chaos holding stacks of clean towels, cleaning supplies, toiletries, and, of course, the endlessly laboring laundry machines. He's checking the room log, his walkie-talkie by his hand, and a disco song about a fever playing. Of course.

"Morning, Cliff. Are Kate's cabins ready?" I ask.

"Ready as Freddie James." He sings a lyric about getting up and boogieing. "But I found suspicious-looking droppings on the front porch."

I wince. "Not again. I thought we got control of the mouse problem last month."

Cliff taps his pen against the log. "Isabel, we're in the mountains surrounded by horse feed, human food, and harsh conditions. Those rodents will do what they got to do to survive. Like all of us."

I close my eyes. It's too early in the morning to be thinking of rodent droppings. "Please call the pest control company again."

"Already done. Left a message."

"Thanks . . . I'll let you know when Ms. Jordan gets here, in case she needs anything else."

We'd placed several last-minute special orders for her dietary requirements, procured a special blow dryer, and found something called an electromagnetic field meter. None of us have a clue why she needs to measure the ranch's electromagnetic field, but as of yesterday, there's one in her room.

"How are your subscriber numbers on YouTube this week?" I ask.

His face lights up. "I covered *Saturday Night Fever* last week, but with this amazing funk beat, and it went bacterial."

"Bacterial?"

"That's just a few hundred-thousand views short of viral."

I laugh. "Keep at it. You'll make post-modern-disco history before long. I believe in you."

"Thanks, Isa. That means a lot to me." He claps his hands and spins. "Disco will never die!"

I walk from housekeeping to the activity center, which includes the kids' camp area, game room, and movie theater, where we show everything from classic westerns in the summers to holiday movies in December. *Elf* was a fan favorite last year. Do A-list Hollywood actresses watch a lot of films? Kate hasn't requested a private screening of anything, but I wouldn't rule it out.

Outside, the dogs sniff around the Kissing Bridge. Three

bridges span the creek from the common buildings to the south to the cabins to the north. Only one of them is named.

The Kissing Bridge was where a young Tom Richardson proposed to an even younger Betty back in 1964. The structure itself isn't anything special, just an ordinary wooden walking bridge over the creek, but Tom and Betty encouraged guests to write their own anonymous love notes on small pieces of paper and put them in a covered basket hanging on the bridge. We post them in the lodge where guests try to guess which one came from their partner. It's a sweet tradition and one of the little draws to the ranch that we think makes us special.

"Zap, don't drink that!"

I shoo the dogs away from the stream. They only recently kicked the Giardia they had earlier in the summer thanks to the medicine that Dr. Travis called in for us last month. They contract the lovely gastrointestinal illness, involving frequent bouts of aromatic diarrhea and vomiting, from drinking creek water teeming with wild animal feces. And because we can't control wild animals, the dogs can get it again and again. Joy.

Maybe Tobias has a point about a dude ranch being no place for three small, energetic dachshunds. As soon as I think that, I scowl. That man can kiss my electromagnetic field reader.

I call Addie on the walkie-talkie. "Everything good in the kitchen?"

Her voice scrambles for a second but then clears. "Wanda's not happy about being a special order vegan chef for one guest, but she's ready."

"Is Myra okay?" She'd cut herself chopping vegetables yesterday. Not for the first time, Cliff had driven her to urgent care after work to be checked out.

"Yes, she's fine. She's working on the green bowl for Kate's lunch."

At least Bianca the psychic is happy to choose from Wanda's daily menu.

"Sounds good. I'm going to check in with the wranglers."

Addie cheers. "Finally!"

Shame washes over me. Somehow, I'd managed to find excuses not to apologize to Tobias. We'd avoided seeing each other without others around, for the most part, over the last few weeks since he started work. I really should own up to being unprofessional that first day. Maybe start building a bridge of understanding between us.

No time like the present, right?

While trudging toward the barn, I use my phone camera to check my teeth from breakfast and plaster on an oatmeal-free smile as I approach the paddock fence. The wranglers, Tobias, Wayne, and Amanda, groom horses inside.

I have to admit I'm impressed with Tobias' work ethic so far. He doesn't need to be doing all of the hands-on work.

He manages the herd, the barn, and the riding program. He'll make short appearances with the guests before rides, during the weekly wagon or sleigh ride, at the big barbecue night, and at the always popular fireside sing-along, where the wranglers make s'mores with the guests, read cowboy poetry, and sing. I hope he has a decent voice.

As I watch him brush a horse down, he certainly looks the part of a handsome cowboy with his long and strong build, tanned skin, and deep-set blue eyes that seem to take the measure of you in one glance.

I could imagine guests being smitten by him . . . if he never opened his mouth.

Tobias cleans the brushes and combs while Wayne and Amanda guide the horses into the stables. After a steadying breath, I duck through the fence. Tobias glances at me and then waves an angry arm.

"Keep those dogs away!"

I hadn't noticed the Zs following me. Zoom jogs in the direction of the horses, which glance at him nervously. The horses are familiar with the dogs, but as a safety precaution, we keep them away. When I call him, he immediately turns back.

Tobias' face is a mottled red as he stalks over to me. I brace. Here we go again.

He keeps his voice low enough that the other wranglers can't hear him. "I've told you about those dogs. They can injure a horse, a guest, or my wranglers. I don't want them near my barn."

I struggle to keep my face neutral. He's absolutely right, but his patronizing, holier-than-thou attitude chafes like wet denim. I swallow what I really want to say and lift my chin up.

"I'm sorry. It won't happen again."

He pushes his hat back on his head, glaring at the Zs, then at me. "See that it doesn't."

"I just said it wouldn't." My words clip off like Nonna dead-heading roses in the garden.

"Good. Then what did you need?"

I'd planned to apologize for my behavior. Truly. But it's not physically possible now. This man makes me livid in body parts I didn't know I could feel.

I unclench my jaw. "To make sure you're ready for Ms. Jordan's arrival."

He flaps an impatient hand. "I know she's an important guest, but I don't plan to treat her any different than anyone else. I'll personally make sure she has a horse that fits her size and temperament, I'll train her up if she needs it, and she and her guests will have a good time. But she'll obey the rules of the trail, or she won't ride."

Part of me—a far distant part—respects that, but I won't be caught dead telling him so. I nod curtly. "Good. She arrives at noon."

I call the Zs to my side, a command they immediately obey, and we leave. So much for bridges.

The next few hours pass quickly; noon comes and goes with no sign of Kate Jordan.

Addie sticks her head in the office, where I've been checking and double-checking the accounts payable software.

We could really use an office manager, but we can't afford one yet.

"Axel texted. Kate wanted to have lunch at a place her friend told her about in Denver. She'll be here at two now."

I keep an eye on the clock, but I needn't have bothered. Kate doesn't arrive at two, at three, or even by dinner.

Addie and I check in again at eight o'clock over a late meal. She looks as tired as I feel. "So, it sounds like Bianca convinced Kate to stop at the Naropa Institute in Boulder for a yoga and mindfulness session. Then, Kate met a friend unexpectedly for dinner. Axel says nine o'clock."

I take a bite of the green bowl Wanda made for Kate's lunch this morning. Delicious. Might as well not let it go to waste.

"Nine tonight? Or in the morning?" The snark is strong in my voice.

An hour later, as the sun sinks behind the mountains to the west, a sleek black SUV pulls into the parking lot of the ranch. Addie and I are going over last month's numbers in the office when we hear the gravel crunching under the tires. We hurry out.

The driver emerges from behind the wheel and heads to the back to unload bags. After him, a woman with jet-black hair pushed back by a colorful scarf steps from the passenger seat. She wears a long, flowing print dress, a chunky knit cardigan, sandals, and a voluminous, cross-body fabric bag. This has to be Bianca the psychic. Kate's golden blonde hair is famous.

Bianca nods to us and then pulls a lighter and what looks like weeds from the bag. She lights the ends of the stalks and, facing the ranch, chants and waves them in a large circle in front of her. I glance at Addie. She shrugs back.

After what feels like ten awkward minutes, the psychic finishes her juju and, with the sun completely behind the peaks now, a thin woman slides out of the back seat, a small dog in her arms.

Queen Kate has arrived.

Chapter Ten

✿❧✿

Isabel

I step toward Kate, extending a hand and my most friendly smile. "Welcome to Lazy Dog Ranch, Ms. Jordan. I'm—"

Kate shakes her head, making me stutter to a stop. "Just a moment, please."

As Bianca extinguishes the weeds and the driver waits patiently with the luggage, the actress tips her chin down to her chest as if in prayer. Addie and I exchange another glance, but what can we do? We wait, too.

Kate isn't particularly dressed like a celebrity. She wears a baseball hat, sunglasses, skinny jeans, and elaborately stitched cowboy boots. I never would have recognized her behind the hat and glasses. The dog, I realize, is a dappled miniature dachshund with luxurious long hair. It sniffs its mistress' cheek while she prays or meditates or maybe takes a catnap.

After about thirty seconds, Kate lifts her head and vaguely smiles at us, as if saying, *Oh, were you waiting for me?*

I introduce Addie and myself. Kate nods at us but doesn't

say anything else. We then shake hands with Bianca. The psychic smells of patchouli and greets us with a solemn Namaste.

"Adorable doxie," Addie remarks to Kate.

"This is Ace." The actress ruffles the dog's fur.

Cautiously, I reach out to let Ace sniff my hand. He gazes at my fingers like he's not sure what I expect him to do. "We have dachshunds on the ranch, too." I look for the Zs; usually, they're right underfoot. "They're around somewhere."

"Well, are you two hungry?" Addie sounds as bright and cheerful as ever. I don't know how she manages it. "Or would you like to go straight to your cabins?"

Kate puts Ace on the ground, where he immediately lifts his tiny leg on the wheel of the SUV.

"I need a few minutes to gather myself if you don't mind."

The actress doesn't say it in a snooty or demanding way. In fact, her voice is kind of dreamy, like she's half-asleep. She ambles toward the lodge.

"Where would you like these?" The driver asks me. From his tone, he's clearly ready to get out of here. Normally, we'd have Phil, our maintenance man-slash-valet, unload and deliver bags for guests, but I told him to go home two hours ago.

"I'll get the Jeep," Addie says, meaning the ranch vehicle that staff uses to shuttle guests, bags, and other necessary things around the property. Our 10,000 acres is a lot of ground to cover. She heads off to the far end of the parking lot.

Ace noses around the parking lot and I wonder again where the Zs are. Axel never told us Kate would bring a dog—not that we would have said no. If she'd informed us she would bring a chupacabra that might suck the blood of half the goats in Boulder County, we probably would have agreed.

"I apologize for our late arrival." Bianca watches Kate wander along the creek. "We didn't feel our original arrival time was conducive to Ms. Jordan's spiritual well-being."

I don't know what to say to that. "We're very glad you made

it. Thank you for choosing Lazy Dog Ranch. Can I ask how you heard about us?"

"Google," Bianca says without any trace of humor. "Ms. Jordan believes in having new, authentic experiences in her time away from work. And she tries to choose venues that aren't already well known. She prides herself in not following the crowd."

I sigh to myself. While I'm glad Kate's spiritual well-being and desire for an authentic experience brought her here, I wish it had been the enthusiastic guest reviews we'd worked hard to gather or our expensive social media campaigns that caught her eye.

Now that I see the psychic's face up close, I realize she has to be at least sixty. Her long, dyed ebony hair and outlandish outfit hide her age well. I'd expect her voice to be soft and dreamy like Kate's, but instead, it's raspy, as if she smokes. I catch a whiff of cigarette smoke behind the patchouli when she swishes her long dress. I'd probably smoke, too, if I worked for a celebrity.

"While Kate's, er, getting acquainted with the ranch, let me tell you the general schedule. We have breakfast from seven to nine, a trail ride at ten, lunch is from eleven-thirty to two, and there's an afternoon ride at three. We have drinks on the patio at five, and dinner is from six to eight. Of course, you're both welcome to do any of the planned activities or none at all, but—"

Wild barking interrupts me. Excusing myself, I hurry that way. By the time I get to the mass of furry bodies beside the Kissing Bridge, my heart is in my throat. The Zs met Ace.

I dive into the writhing dog pile and pluck the smaller dog out of the melee. It's easier than corralling the other three on my own. The Zs bark excitedly, wanting him back. Teeth bared and a growl rippling from his throat, Ace struggles to get down again.

I examine the little dog as Kate hurries over to me. "I'm so sorry," I say. "Our dogs aren't used to having new dogs here."

Kate's eyebrows crimp with worry. "Is he injured?"

I hand Ace to her. "Not that I can tell."

"Are you all right, *mon petit chou?*" She looks him over. "He seems fine. Just a little . . . wet."

The Zs' tongues loll proudly. I apologize again. "We'll do our best to keep them on a leash while Ace is here."

"That seems prudent all the time." Bianca huffs, her pale face disapproving. "I sense discontent."

I'm tempted to roll my eyes at her. The dogs are all still growling at each other, so, yeah, I sense discontent, too.

"Maybe we can introduce them again in the morning." Then again, maybe not. It was almost a doxie disaster.

Kate nuzzles Ace and makes a noncommittal sound.

"Can I show you to your cabins now?" Desperation coats my words. Without waiting for an answer, I lead the way.

As we cross the bridge, I wrack my brain for small talk that will erase Kate's memory of her pet being mugged by the Zs.

I consider casual questions like, How's Los Angeles? Who are you dating now that you broke up with what's-his-name? Were the rumors true that you once sat all day without speaking inside a giant fake sprinkled donut outside a Hollywood donut shop?

"Do you have tea?" Bianca asks.

I answer gratefully. "Yes, all our rooms are equipped with a coffee pod machine that can also make tea."

She shakes her head. "No, no. I need the leaves. For a reading."

A . . . reading? It's nine-thirty at night and they want tea leaves for a reading? Wanda and Myra put together an assortment of light snacks for Kate and Bianca before they left, but I have no idea where to find loose leaf tea. If we even have any. And shouldn't a psychic carry her own tealeaf stash for emergency readings?

My gratitude turns to annoyance, which I work hard to cover. "I'll go look in the kitchen. I think we have English breakfast."

The psychic shudders. "No, no. Black tea creates dark prophecies. I prefer oolong or green but white will do."

Okay. If my father, a biochemist, were here, he'd be rolling on the ground laughing by now. He had no tolerance for New Age hocus-pocus.

"I'll see what I can find," I say.

I lead Kate to the Breckenridge cabin, pointing out the different common buildings along the way. The Zs follow us, still barking at Ace in Kate's arms every thirty seconds. I cringe, but it can't be helped. Their leashes are in the office. At least I manage to keep them out of Kate's cabin when we get there.

Addie and the driver have already dropped off Kate's luggage, which sits inside the door. As soon as we enter, Bianca lights a candle from her bag and paces the room with it, chanting again and waving her hands around. I stare, but Kate ignores her.

I show Kate the features of the room, glancing at her anxiously. I hope it's to her liking, but she's still wearing the dark oversized sunglasses so her expression is hard to read. When I finish, I don't know what else to do other than tell her how to reach Addie and me if she needs us.

"Thank you," she says. "I believe this could be a place of peace for me."

Relief pours over me like loose leaf tea. "I certainly hope so, Ms. Jordan. And I'm sorry again about our dogs."

"Call me Kate. Just Kate."

She sets Ace on the bed. The doxie races around in circles before flopping beside the pillows, which he starts to gum, leaving at least a few tooth-sized holes. Bianca's still flapping around like a giant bat. Time to go.

"I'll be outside when you're ready to go to your cabin, Bianca." I wait on the porch for her to finish the incantations.

Addie and the driver are chatting away in the Durango cabin when we get there. As soon as he sees the psychic, though, he takes off with a smile for my friend. My heart pinches. Addie makes friends so easily. Why is it always a struggle for me? We show Bianca around, and she thanks us with a dignified bow.

Once outside, I take a long breath and meet Addie's amused eyes. We break into quiet laughter.

"I don't even know where to start with them," I say.

"What was Bianca doing out there?" Addie swings her hand toward the parking lot.

"I don't know, but she did it in Kate's cabin, too." I head downhill toward the kitchen.

"Where are you going? I'm exhausted."

"I need to find tea leaves for Kate's reading, of course. Do you know if we have any?"

"No idea," Addie says with a long sigh. "But I'll help you try to find it."

"If we have to, we'll empty an oregano container and hope for the best."

"I vote for dried anise," Addie says darkly.

It's been a very long day, and from what I've seen so far of Kate and Bianca, it won't be the last one of their stay. But at least she feels it could be a place of peace for her, whatever that means.

Namaste.

Chapter Eleven

Tobias

The sun spills pools of gold and blue light over the foothills to the east and into the valley as I stroll past the cabins toward the barn. The place really is beautiful. I hope for all our sakes that the actress who arrived late last night, Kate Jordan, agrees.

I think about grabbing a cup of coffee as I pass the kitchen. Wanda and Myra are probably prepping for breakfast. But I decided against it; I want to be sure we're ready for the day.

I'm finally starting to know the people and routines around the ranch. The wait staff has to be up early, ready to serve breakfast, while the housekeepers get a little extra sleep. Cliff will be rallying his staff in the housekeeping office in an hour or so.

I'd met the man a few days after I started. He'd been singing a disco song for an upset kid who'd fallen and skinned her knees in the playground. The funny way he sang it made her laugh, the injury forgotten, and her mom grateful. Cliff was an odd one, I knew, but I liked him.

I turn my eyes to the barn. I got lucky with my staff, too. Wayne and Amanda seem like good people. They should be out in the pasture collecting up the horses I chose for the trail rides today. While they're out, I'll work with Nightrider in the arena. She's a young, headstrong mare who needs more instruction before she's ready to work.

Lost in my thoughts about the day, I almost trip over the woman balancing on her forearms and toes on the ground inside the barn. She's in tight workout clothes doing some kind of yoga pose . . . with a dog on her back. A little dachshund. I grunt to myself. More dogs.

The yogi's eyes are closed. The dog watches me calmly.

I clear my throat. "Excuse me, ma'am, but guests aren't allowed in here alone."

Slowly, the woman lowers her body, the dog with it, to the ground, showing impressive arm and core strength. With her hands planted and arms extended, she raises her head and shoulders into the air, stretching. Once she's back on the ground, the dog steps lightly off her back.

The woman turns over and sits cross-legged, tucking her feet under her legs. She places the palms of her hands together in front of her chest and finally opens her eyes. They're startlingly blue.

"I'm not alone," she says. "You're here."

I blink. There's nothing to say because she's not wrong. I study her. She's a bit skinny, with long, wavy blonde hair up in a bun on her head. She wears no makeup, but her skin is perfect. And I've seen her before.

"Ms. Jordan?" I guess.

Ellen and I watched a movie she was in once, one of those family dramas where everyone has secrets. It wasn't my thing, but Ellen liked it. My heart squeezes, just for a second, thinking of my ex-wife.

"Kate." She tilts her head at the dog. "And this is Ace."

I choose my words carefully, something I've been determined to do since my last tangle with Isa.

"Ma'am, I'm Tobias Coleman, head wrangler. We're all happy you came for a visit, but I have to tell you that it's against barn rules for guests to be here by themselves. And mixing unfamiliar dogs with horses is definitely dangerous."

"Of course. I understand."

Kate unfolds herself smoothly, slips her feet into sandals, rolls up her mat, and brushes off her slim legs. Once she's upright, I realize she's only a few inches shorter than me. Her smile dazzles me a little.

"I'm sorry," she says, "I was led here this morning."

I squint. "Led by who?"

"By my spiritual guides. This felt like the place where I could connect most with my higher power."

"In the barn?" I sniff. If horse manure helps you connect to a higher power, then the barn is your place.

"I go where I'm directed," she says lightly.

I step to the stable door and point. "Beyond the paddock, there's a really nice, flat sunny spot with great views. Maybe you'd be more comfortable exercising there."

She scoops up the dog and walks beside me to see where I mean.

"Thank you. I appreciate the recommendation, and I am sorry we broke the rules."

"No problem. I hope you'll come for a trail ride later today. We run them in the morning and afternoon. But sorry, big guy, no dogs allowed."

I hold out my hand to scratch the dog, but instead, Kate takes my hand in both of hers and . . . sniffs it?

"You smell like kindness, Tobias." Still holding my hand, her mouth reshapes into that sensational smile again. She collects the yoga mat and pads away.

I stare after Kate Jordan as if I've just met an alien—and an alien's dog. After looking around to be sure I'm not being watched, I sniff the same hand.

Smells like Dove soap to me.

This place is more head-scratching by the day, but I'll say this for it: it's far from boring.

Chapter Twelve

✦✦✦

Isabel

Addie and I thought we'd be plenty early for breakfast, leaving time to mingle with our other guests before Kate arrives, but despite her late arrival last night, the actress beats us to it.

She sits alone at a table in a sunny corner of the outside patio, wearing exercise tights and sandals with a sweatshirt, reading a book, drinking a mug of tea and eating slow spoonfuls of amaranth porridge, which Axel informed Addie, who told Wanda, is her favorite morning meal.

Wanda said, "Porridge. Porridge? And just what the hell is *amaranth* porridge?"

None of us knew. We had to look it up on Amazon.

"I wonder why she travels alone," I whisper to Addie as we make our way to her table.

"She's not alone. She has Bianca."

"Yeah, but she's on staff. Can you imagine only traveling with your hired help?"

Addie and I usually travel together, unless we're going on a family trip or if one of us happens to have a boyfriend . . . which neither of us has had since we decided to quit our jobs and buy the ranch. And we haven't had the time—or money—to travel since then.

"I read that she ended a relationship with that Jason Mason guy recently. Maybe she needed alone time."

"Jason Maxon."

"Whatever. The hunky one with the dark hair and muscles."

"Would you want alone time after him?" I ask.

Addie snorts. "I'd want to cry over losing him."

We greet Kate. She says good morning but looks at us like she can't quite place us. With a sigh, I remind her of our names.

"How's your porridge?" Addie asks. "We're very proud of Wanda, our head chef. She does a wonderful job."

Kate sips her tea. "Oh, I'm sure she does, but Bianca made this batch. She knows just how I like it."

Addie and I exchange looks. Not good. Wanda will be in a snit for sure.

"Was your cabin comfortable?" I ask.

She closes her book and considers it. "I slept well. And I had a lovely yoga session with Ace this morning in the barn."

My heart rate picks up. Thank god Tobias didn't see her doing yoga in his barn. And with a dog no less.

"I met the head wrangler," she says. "He was very clear that I shouldn't exercise in the barn anymore."

Panic hammers my chest, but I try to hide it. "I'm sorry if he was rude. It's Tobias' job to keep guests safe and the horses healthy. I can speak to him—"

Kate shakes her head serenely. "He was very nice about it all. He even suggested another spot for tomorrow morning."

"Oh . . . well," I stammer, "that's . . . good." And shocking. *Nice* about it all?

Addie raises an eyebrow at me. "I hope you'll try a trail ride today," she says to Kate. "We're told we have some of the best trails and most beautiful views of any dude ranch in Colorado. Is there anything you need in the meantime?"

"No, but thank you for checking on me." Kate turns back to her book. I notice the title: *The Secret Language of Angels*.

"I'll do the coffee and chat with the guests," Addie says as we walk away. "You better go take Wanda's pulse."

I hurry into the kitchen in time to catch Myra banging the back of her head on the underside of the worktable, where she scrambled to retrieve a dropped utensil. I help her up.

"Are you okay?" I ask. She rubs her head and nods. "*Please* be caref—?"

I stare, speechless, at the stainless steel table surface where something that looks like a bright green chunk of sod sits in a round baking dish. "What is this?"

"Ms. Jordan's lunch. It's an egg casserole thing with a lot of parsley in it. Bianca said parsley is good for balancing the energy flows through the body."

Myra's wide, dark eyes are serious. Her petite frame and thin limbs give her a childlike look, which in turn makes it harder to get frustrated with her when she burns dishes, breaks appliances, and has accidents.

"What's she like?" she asks.

"Bianca?" I think about it. "Well, she's—"

"No—Ms. Jordan." Myra breathes the actress' name like a prayer.

"Nice enough." So far. "Maybe a little odd, but okay. Myra, where's Wanda?"

"Out back. Contemplating."

That's what Wanda always says when she goes outside for her break. *I'm going out to contemplate my life.* The ranch chef sits, legs splayed and apron covering her wide thighs, at a picnic table under a tree. Although it's only eight in the morning, she's smoking a cigarillo. I approach cautiously.

"Everything okay?" I ask.

She points the cigarillo up the hill at the cabins. "That woman does *not* get to call the shots in my kitchen."

I put my hands together and sit beside her. This will take some work. "Wanda, I'm sorry Ms. Jordan sent her staff in to make her breakfast. That was rude and presumptuous and—"

"Not her, I'm talking about that she-spider, Bianca." She spits on the ground beside her. "Ms. Jordan requires this, Ms. Jordan will only eat that. Ms. Jordan takes her tea in this way. Ms. Jordan has a special recipe for that. Ms. Jordan can kiss my big, white—"

I hold up my hands. "I understand you're frustrated, Wanda. But remember what I told you all in the staff meeting before she arrived." My voice lowers. "No matter what she does or says, it's our job to makes sure she loves her stay and shares that love with her friends, family, and fans. We *need* this."

Wanda heaves a long sigh and stubs out her cigar in an ashtray. "I know, which is why I didn't throw her boneheaded butt out of my kitchen that instant. Sorry, Isa. It's just that between Myra being Myra, a crash course in vegan cooking, and the psychic taking over my kitchen, I'm tearing my hair out. Really, look." She points to a tuft of her gray hair traveling in a gentle breeze by her feet.

I touch her arm. "Hang in there, Wanda. We'll all have to work hard to make these next two weeks successful. If we pull it off and get lots of new reservations out of it, maybe we can relax soon."

Wanda nods. "You and Addie keep up the good work. You know we're rooting for you. It took guts to come up here and make a go of this with no experience. You two have guts in spades." She makes a fist like Rosie the Riveter.

Genuine tears actually jump to my eyes. "Thank you, Wanda, that means a lot. We wouldn't be able to do anything without you and your amazing cooking."

Her nicotine-stained smile is disarmingly girlish. "It is amazing ain't it? My cooking and my Cory are my pride and joy.

Oh, hey, while I'm thinking on it, can I make an announcement about Cory's charity show in the next staff meeting?"

"Of course."

Wanda's son, who she calls her *aspiring* rock star, is organizing a show with his classic rock band to raise money for the local volunteer fire department, which he's also a part of. How you can still *aspire* to a rock and roll career at age forty, I'm not sure, but Addie and I agreed to sponsor the event to help support the community, something we've been trying to do since we got here.

My walkie-talkie crackles. It's Addie. "Hey, do you have a minute? I think we have a problem."

My stomach clenches. *Dio Santo.* No more problems. "Where are you? I'll come to you."

"Meet me on the Kissing Bridge."

"Thank you for feeding us all so well despite the distractions, Wanda."

"That she-spider is a nightmare, not a distraction." With a final grunt, she heads back into the kitchen to wash her hands, I hope.

Addie leans against the rail of the bridge as I approach.

"What's up?" Trepidation flickers through my body. How many fires will we have to put out before this place runs smoothly?

"Don't be obvious, but do you see the pair sitting on the patio having drinks a few tables away from Kate?" Addie nods toward a man and a woman in their late 30s. I glance over.

"The Devitas?" They'd checked in two days ago. So far they've kept to themselves, not joining in with the trail rides or after dinner activities. Which wasn't all that unusual. Some of our guests come strictly to relax.

"Cliff told me they have a lot of expensive camera equipment in their room, but no one on staff has seen them taking pictures of the ranch or the view or anything so far."

I make a face. "So?"

"So, Jamie just told me—"

"Jamie the waitress or Jamie the kid wrangler?"

"Waitress. She said she saw them up on the porch of their cabin taking a bunch of pictures of Kate having breakfast, then they went down there, without the cameras, and sat a few tables away as if nothing happened."

I shrug. "She's a celebrity. Lots of people will probably want pictures of her once they realize she's here."

"But then, why would they have all that equipment? And why would they take the pictures from far away instead of taking selfies or something?" Addie leans in, eyes wide. "Cliff thinks they're paparazzi."

I study the couple. They aren't even looking at Kate. "Addie, you know you love a mystery."

And her partner in crime is usually Cliff. In the last eighteen months, the two of them suspected one of the college staff was moonlighting as a stripper in Boulder (not true. Confirmed by Cory and Wayne on a joint reconnaissance mission they were happy to take.). They also thought a contractor who was here to fix the ranch's generators really worked for the National Security Agency and came to bug the ranch (also not true, at least as far as we could determine). And last but not least, they thought Wanda was having an affair with old Doc Garner, the veterinarian, which, when Wanda got wind of the rumor, she squelched in short order. Although, she admitted she had a fling with him back in high school.

"Then what are they doing with all that equipment?" she asks.

"I don't know, but I do know that having cameras isn't illegal." I sigh. "Addie, what will we do about it even if they are paparazzi? They're paying customers and so far they haven't prompted a complaint from Kate."

"I think we should watch out for them." She chews on her lip. "If you notice anything, let me know."

"I will. But there won't be anything to notice. The Devitas are here to enjoy a vacation, just like Kate."

Then again . . . I'll keep my eye on the couple. The last thing we need right now is a scandal involving our most important guest yet.

Chapter Thirteen

✦✦✦

Tobias

I'm mucking out stalls, one of the many glamorous jobs of a wrangler, when Wayne and Amanda finish their lunch break and show up to help. I don't really mind the physical work—it helps me not to think so much—but it's good to have company. I stop shoveling and wipe my forehead and neck with the bandana I have shoved in my back pocket.

"Hey, boss," Wayne says. "That actress and her fortuneteller are coming on the ride today."

My forehead wrinkles. "Fortune teller?"

Amanda grins. She's about thirty-five and from another local ranching family. Good people, from what I hear from my dad.

"She has a psychic with her. Wanda calls her the she-spider, but her name is Bianca."

She-spider? I shrug a shoulder. "Well, whatever. Let's make sure all the horses are ready to go."

"On it," Wayne says.

My cell phone vibrates in my pocket. I wipe my hands off

and pull it out to read the text from my mom. Actually, it's from Tyler.

guess what dad i got invited to a birthday party

I write back. *That's great bud. Whose?*

A girl named hallie or holly or something

I chuckle. *How'd you meet her?*

i didnt. shes grandpas friends granddaughter. shes in another class

We write back and forth a few more times before I put the phone away again. But my chest feels full. Tyler hasn't been to a party or made a friend since we moved back from Wyoming two months ago. He wants to have a party for his birthday in early October, but I don't know who he'll invite after only being in school for a few weeks.

I wouldn't know who to invite to a party either, now that I think about it. Most of my friends growing up have moved away, and I haven't had time to catch up with the few that stuck around since I got back.

I whistle as I work, thinking about Tyler making some new friends, and maybe getting back into playing T-ball. He played before but had to stop when his symptoms got worse.

I finish mucking and go to wash up in the small stable bathroom. The trail riders are supposed to be here early for the three o'clock ride, but my experience with guests who have a late lunch with a drink or two is that they'll be late. And the last to arrive is Kate Jordan and the fortuneteller, Bianca.

I touch my hat to them. Kate's dressed in a fitted plaid shirt, the skinny kind of jeans that tuck into her scuffed riding boots, and a hat. She looks ready to ride off in a Hollywood western.

But the other woman—Bianca. I can't quite keep from staring. She wears a long, flowing dress that trails on the ground behind her and an almost as long chunky sweater, although it's warm out today. Her dark hair is swept up in a huge messy pile on her head with a bright scarf doing its best to keep it all up there. I look down, but I can't see her feet under all the clothes.

"Ma'am, I'm sorry, but I need to be sure you have on appropriate footwear."

With a wink, she lifts the hem of her dress a bit so I can see her rainbow-colored ankle-high sneaker boots. They do have a heel, although they're not exactly what we mean when we recommend heeled boots or shoes in the guests' packing list.

I remember what the head wrangler told me the first day of my first wrangling job: a trail ride is only as safe as its weakest rider. I suppress a sigh. Ladies and gents, we found our weakest rider.

Using my guest list, I greet the rest of the guests, about eight in all. At other ranches, we'd have twelve or more and maybe even a second group going a half-hour later.

"Wayne will lead your ride today," I tell them. "Let us know if you're having any trouble at all as we get you settled. If you'll follow us over here, we'll introduce you to your horse for the week."

Wayne and Amanda start pairing guests with horses. They help the riders mount and then walk around checking stirrups and tightening cinches while Amanda gives the group the basic riding instructions.

I take Kate and Bianca. They'd be fine with either of my wranglers, but in a staff meeting before the actress arrived I had strict instructions to look after them myself.

"Ms. Jordan," I say, "this is Sagebrush. I think you two will get along fine."

Kate greets Sage, a sweet little paint, by letting the horse sniff her palm and then petting the mare's face.

"Hello, toby," she says.

I startle at the use of my mother's nickname before I realize Kate's talking to the mare. Paints have different color patterns, and Sage is a tobiano or a toby for short. She's brown and white, with the white traveling up her legs and over her back, while her head is brown with a white star on the forehead.

"You know about horses." I can't help sounding surprised.

She smiles. "I rode growing up."

"Where was that?"

"In California. Ventura County."

She gets a dreamy look on her face—although she always looks that way now that I think about it. I'd planned to bring a stepstool over to Sage's side, but instead, I offer her my laced hands to step into. She grips the horn and slides easily into the saddle.

I move to help Bianca mount her Appaloosa, Azure, but the older woman has already hoisted herself up—dress, sweater, rainbow sneakers and all. I'm impressed.

A man, named Devita according to the list, struggles to mount Parker. The horse drifts sideways, tossing his mane and giving the stink eye to the human trying to get into the saddle from the wrong side. I hurry over to the man, who has a fancy camera secured with a strap across his chest.

"Hang on, come around to his left side." I show Devita how to hold the reins, and then I guide his shiny new boot into the stirrup. After hopping a few times, he gets up, already sweating. Luckily, Parker is patient.

Amanda helps a heavily made-up woman in head to toe pink with jeweled boots onto her horse. "Hang on, Ms. Hamilton, you've got the wrong foot in the stirrup."

"C'mon, Mom, hurry up. You're embarrassing yourself," her young teenaged daughter says. Rudely, in my opinion.

Another guest squeaks when her horse swats hard at a fly with its tail, batting her in the leg. I know from experience that it doesn't hurt, but it can startle. Wayne steps to her horse and speaks to the woman, his calm hand on the bridle. Her frightened expression turns to a smile.

Meanwhile, Bianca leads Azure around in comfortable circles. Hmm, I might've misjudged the weakest link.

"All right, time to head out." Wayne lays his cowpoke accent on thick. He's a horseman to be sure, but he's from New York—not exactly the Wild West.

I head back to Kate. "All well?"

"Yes, but aren't you coming?"

I spot Addie at the paddock fence, watching. "No ma'am, I don't lead the trail rides most days."

"No need to call me ma'am or Ms. Jordan. I'm Kate. And . . . maybe you can make an exception one of these times." Her voice holds a flirtatious note.

I glance at the actress, but I'm focused on catching Addie before she leaves. "Yes, ma'am, Kate, I'll see what I can do."

Amanda instructs the riders to follow the horse in front single file out of the paddock. The mounts are all well trained; they know what to do, but I keep an eye on the group anyway as I walk over to Addie.

"Thanks for making sure Ms. Jordan and her friend were comfortable," she says.

"No problem. It's my job." I lean against the fence, and we watch until the riders and horses walk over a ridge and out of sight.

"How are things going for you, Tobias?" Addie asks. "Are you settling in okay?"

I nod. "Wayne and Amanda are hard workers, and they care about the horses, the guests, and their jobs. Which is more than I can say for others I've worked with over the years. The herd is a bit small but in good shape. We'll need to talk about ordering some new materials and equipment this year. Some of the fencing is wearing out, and the tractor's on its last legs. The stables are also going to need a few repairs." She looks pale, so I add, "Not everything has to be done right away. I'm just taking stock."

"Okay, Isa and I will set up a meeting with you soon to discuss what's needed."

I tap my hand against the railing and take a breath. I've got a lot of things to do before the riders get back, but first, I need to get this off my chest, even if it's to the wrong person.

"Speaking of Isa, I don't feel like we got off on the right foot.

I want to clear the air, but every time I talk to her, we seem to argue."

Addie nods. "Oh, the stories I could tell you. Isa is a fiery woman, but under her quick temper, she cares about this place and her employees." She nudges me and grins. "Even you." She pitches her voice lower. "And she knows she owes you an apology."

Surprised, I blink. Not that I disagree we both have things to feel bad about, I just doubted Isa would bend enough to admit it.

"Any suggestions of how I can talk to her that won't end with her yelling insults at me?"

She smiles sheepishly. "That's one of the things she's sorry about." She thinks, her mouth twisting. "Your best bet is a straightforward request for a fresh start. What about at the campfire this afternoon? You'll be there, right? Maybe you can find a minute to talk to her."

"Okay, I'll try, but listen, don't tell her I spoke to you. I don't want her to think I'm talking about her behind her back."

"Don't worry, she's talking behind your back, too." She smiles again. "This is a good idea, Tobias. Once you two start over, you'll see Isa's a real sweetheart. One of the best."

I make a face. Isa a sweetheart?

"Seriously, she's been my rock over the last ten years. But you have to take the bad with the good with people you love sometimes."

Ellen's face floats into my mind, but I shake off the memories of my ex. "Thanks, Addie. Good talk."

"Good luck, Tobias."

I push off the fence and head toward the stables to repair some tack, already thinking about what I can say to get back on good terms with Isa.

I'd be happy with an apology, a handshake, and one of her smiles. But given our history, that might be too much to ask.

Chapter Fourteen

✺

Isabel

A highlight of my day is meeting Cliff for an update. He keeps me posted about furniture, decor, supplies, or repairs needed for the cabins, anything Phil fixed or is working on, and of course, a preview of his newest YouTube video.

"Then I do kind of a West Coast hustle move," he taps his foot out in a semi-circle and swings around, "and end with a modified slide." He slips across the housekeeping office floor and blinds me with a huge smile.

"It looks great," I say. "Can you tell how the video's doing yet?"

"No, I never check my numbers at work. Too busy." He smirks.

"Sure you don't. All right, I have to get to the campfire, so drive safe and have a good night, okay?"

"Will do." Cliff hums to himself as he switches off the computer and grabs his car keys. He drives a newish Mercedes and lives somewhere around Boulder, although no one at the ranch, even staff like Wayne or Wanda who has been here a long time, knows much else about him.

Cliff doesn't talk about family, partners, lovers, roommates, or much of anything other than his YouTube channel and his obsession with disco and funk. He has a two-track mind: work and music. Wayne says he's a lucky man. All I know is his good cheer never fails to lift my own spirits.

He heads to the staff parking lot as I walk to the campfire area below the dining room patio. It's a cleared space with a sizable fire pit and comfortable chairs all around.

I take a quick bathroom break in my office, splash water on my face, and brush my hair, which is loose today. I'd love to skip the campfire and go straight to bed, but the guests, not to mention our staff, expect me to be there.

We have two kinds of campfires, this late afternoon one, when guests grab drinks, relax their saddle-sore backsides and mingle. Wanda's son Cory sometimes plays the guitar. The other kind is the after-dinner campfire when the wranglers recite cowboy poetry and lead songs, while the kid wranglers corral the children to make s'mores and play games.

We usually have a few campfires a week, with another night reserved for the evening hayride. The majority of the staff, including Addie and me, generally has Friday nights off, which also happens to be movie night for the guests.

I smile and greet guests as I arrive, asking about their days. Addie's already here . . . and so is Tobias. I try not to look at him, although I can feel his eyes on me.

"It was so exciting to be on a trail ride with Kate Jordan," one of the guests, Sharon Hamilton from Miami, Florida, gushes. I have a hard time not smiling at her pink denim outfit—with fringe. "She's a very good rider. When the wrangler asked if anyone felt comfortable taking the lead for a few minutes, Kate was the first to volunteer! Jim and I had no idea we'd be visiting the ranch with a celebrity. We've been sharing pictures of her all afternoon on Facebook."

"I'm so happy you're having a good time," I say sincerely. And I hope she tagged all those Facebook pictures with the Lazy Dog Ranch's location.

But I feel a little sorry for Kate. She can't be happy about strangers documenting practically every moment of her day. On the other hand, she chose to vacation on a ranch where she knew regular people would be. Maybe she doesn't mind.

As I'm thinking this, Kate, Bianca, and Ace appear. The other guests whisper and stare as the actress, the psychic, and the mini doxie take seats in the circle. Jamie the waitress hurries to bring them drinks. Bianca takes one, but Kate shakes her head. She snuggles Ace and stares at the fire, seeming oblivious to the attention.

Addie greets them, speaking to the women with smiles and laughter like she's visiting old friends. I feel a twinge of jealousy while watching her. How does she pull off being so natural, no matter who she's with?

Sharon hustles over to her husband and tween daughter to point out Kate to them, and someone new touches my elbow. I turn to greet whoever it is with a smile, but my expression hardens when I see who it is.

Get a grip, Isa. It's time to bury the hatchet with Tobias. I can't afford to not get along with someone so important to the ranch. I need to put our differences behind me. Although . . . when I picture burying that hatchet with Tobias, I decide it might not be the safest metaphor.

I greet him, keeping my tone upbeat. "How are things at the barn?"

"Well enough." He crosses his arms and looks across the campfire to where Cory's started to play an acoustic guitar.

I nod, not sure how to start. It doesn't help that he looks as uncomfortable as I feel. He keeps glancing at me sideways, but he doesn't speak.

After a long breath, my words come out in a rush. "Tobias, I think . . . I think I owe you an apology. We didn't start off well, and I know at least part of that was my fault. I'm sorry for how I spoke to you on your first day and for slamming the door on you."

His expression doesn't change. "What about the name you called me?"

"No, I meant that," I smirk at his shocked expression. "Seriously, though, I hope we can put our first few meetings behind us and start fresh."

He scuffs the side of his boot against the ground. "I don't know. I'm not sure that's possible."

I brush a strand of hair out of my face. "I don't understand."

"I mean, I don't think I can accept your apology."

I stiffen. "And why not?"

"Because I—"

"Tobias . . ." Kate beckons him from her seat, pulling her soft golden waves over one shoulder. She pats the bench beside her.

"Go ahead," I say stiffly.

Tobias looks from her to me. "She can wait. I want to finish what I was saying."

"I think you already made it very clear."

"Isa, I . . ." He sighs. "Never mind. I'll see you later."

He looks unhappy about it, but he joins Kate, who immediately leans into his shoulder. He sits stiffly at first, his hands on his knees, but after a minute his body relaxes, and they laugh together. Maybe there's a method to Kate's solo vacation madness.

My temples pulse with irritation. I don't know how he can possibly justify not accepting an apology. Especially when I find them so hard to produce. The wrangler and I are just not meant to get along. That's all there is to it.

I move into a shadowy corner to try and calm down. Watching the guests helps. Bianca stands by the snack table seeming to consult the stars over whether she should have a brisket slider or cut vegetables and hummus. The brisket wins out.

Addie's chatting with a nice couple from New Mexico, the Pérezes, while their teenage son can't stop gawking at Kate. Wayne regales a family with a story about a trail ride interrupted by a freak thunderstorm years ago that had the horses bucking riders and racing for the barn. I'm sure it wasn't funny at the time, but even their tween daughters laugh as he tells the tale now.

I smooth my shirt, wishing I had funny stories to tell or at least a charming personality like Addie. Even stern Tobias is popular. Maybe I should chain myself to my desk in the back office and spend my time stressing over spreadsheets instead. But when Addie waves me over, I reluctantly go.

"Have you met my co-owner Isa yet?" My friend asks the Pérezes. She puts her arm around me. "She is the toughest, most generous, most hardworking woman on the planet. Isa can create magic with a spreadsheet, prepare a mean *spaghetti carbonara*, and plunge a toilet with the best of them."

They smile and say hello as I hug Addie back with tears in my eyes. Somehow she always knows the right thing to say right when I need to hear it. I guess that's what best friends are for.

I wipe my cheeks quickly when I see Tobias looking. Perfect. The last thing I want is for him to see me crying.

"And *this*," I say, "is the most even-keeled, loving, and dedicated woman in the universe. Addie can sell a plot of land to a fish, sweet-talk a raincloud out of the sky, and convince three mischievous dachshunds not to knock over the kitchen trashcan even if there *are* meat scraps inside."

As we chat, my attention catches on the Devitas. They stand away from the group, admiring the scenery. The woman, Laura, points at the mountains lit up in the golden hour sun, but the man, Marshall, seems to be taking pictures of the group with an unobtrusive camera. Wait, not the group—Kate and Tobias.

I glance over at them. The actress' lips are almost nuzzling

Tobias' ear. His body language seems stiff again, but he chuckles at whatever she said. When I look back at the Devitas, they're gazing at the mountains, no camera in sight.

Chapter Fifteen

Tobias

Isa and Addie call a lunchtime staff meeting the day after the disastrous campfire. Lunch is one of the few hours of the day that most of us are on duty. I take my seat in the staff room, a cramped space near the housekeeping office, alongside Wayne, Amanda, and a few others

Cliff comes in and sits beside me singing *Funky Town* using a new handheld shower sprayer, tags still on. He sits beside me with a huff and crosses his arms over his chest.

"I love our boss ladies, but these staff meetings give me a pain in my trunk. I've got things to do, you know?"

I snort in agreement. I did know. The barn was in chaos this morning after we discovered one of the horses has strangles, a contagious respiratory disease. He had to be isolated, Doc Garner called, and the rest of the herd checked for symptoms. On top of everything we normally do. The ranch could really use another wrangler, but I doubt now's the time to tell Isa and Addie that.

The owners come in, leashed Zs in tow, and stand at the front of the room, waiting for us to settle down. I study Isa as she asks the dogs to lie down. Damn. She's entirely too beautiful for someone I don't get along with.

I try to catch her eye, but she's obviously pretending I'm not sitting two rows in front of her. Frustrated, I jam my hands in my pockets. I haven't had this much trouble with a woman since . . . well, ever. I kicked myself the whole drive home last night for not finishing what I'd planned to say to Isa before Kate summoned me.

The actress was nice enough, but she seems to have decided I should be her companion when she's bored with Bianca, even going so far as to invite me to join her for a meal in the dining room last night.

I'd politely declined. Tyler had made dinner for the first time with Mom's help—homemade mac and cheese—and I wasn't about to miss it, even for an invitation from a movie star.

Isa starts the meeting with a few reminders about keeping the staff room clean and being on time to shifts, and an announcement reminding us about the charity event at the Rock n' Roll Bar. Then she gets down to business.

"We've made a discovery in a guest room that we need to make you all aware of."

"Drugs?" A waiter says.

"Porn?" A waitress asks to laughter.

Isa rolls her eyes. "No. Camera equipment."

"For making porn?" The waitress says.

"It's nothing to do with porn!" Addie says. "At least, as far as we know. But the equipment looks professional."

"Like paparazzi might have," Cliff finishes dramatically.

That's greeted by silence, and then some interested whispering.

"We've seen Laura and Marshall Devita taking pictures of Kate and," Isa shoots a look at me, then away, "members of our staff the last few days. We aren't sure what they're up to, but we want you all to let Addie or me know if you see them breaking any ranch rules. As of now, other than letting Ms. Jordan know what we've observed, we don't think there's much else we can do."

Dale the housekeeper raises his hand. "How do you know they aren't just nosy people? Wanting pictures to show their friends or whatever."

"I did some snooping online myself," Addie says, "and I found a picture of the Devitas in an article about paparazzi based in Los Angeles."

"Maybe she knows who they are, then," Amanda says.

"We'll find out when we speak to her," Addie says.

Given the look Isa sent my way, the Devitas must have taken pictures of Kate and me, maybe at the campfire. Would they be published?

I guess it isn't a big deal. I can explain the situation to my folks. Tyler's probably too young to hear about it. Any friends that see the pictures will give me hell about it, but nothing I can't handle.

"We'll let you know if anything changes," Isa says. "For now, keep an eye out and, of course, please respect her privacy as well as the privacy of all our guests. This isn't a witch-hunt.

Everyone stands. I try to catch Isa, but Wanda gets to her first, gesturing and talking angrily about a spider.

I figure I'll wait them out. The weenies look up at me expectantly, and in a moment of weakness, I lean over to pet them. Their tails go nuts and all three try to press their soft heads into my hand at once. I squat down, which really gets them going. They put their stubby front legs on my knee, sending me off balance.

I give each of them a good rub, which they seem to appreciate judging by the way they flop on their backs so I can reach their bellies easier. When I look up again, Isa is watching me. She moves her eyes away quickly.

I check my watch. Wanda doesn't seem to be slowing

anytime, and I need to get back to the barn. Maybe I should make an appointment.

The frustration I'm feeling must show on my face because Addie pats my arm sympathetically as I go by.

"Hey," I ask, "were those Devita people taking my picture with Kate?"

Her lips thin. "We think so."

"Nothing illegal about pictures in public, I guess."

She nudges my arm. "It must be hard work to cozy up to a famous Hollywood actress."

She's teasing me so I laugh, but I've never been one to care about fame. I'm happy to be friendly with Kate if it helps the ranch, and if someone wants to take pictures of us, so be it.

Now if only I could pin down that prickly *other* supervisor of mine and get her to smile.

That, I'd like a picture of.

Chapter Sixteen

Isabel

Addie and I ask to meet Kate later that day at her cabin. When we get there, Bianca's on the front porch overlooking the valley. It's a peaceful spot, especially as the moon comes up and the ranch quiets down.

The psychic is in all black. Black sweater, pants, and sandals. She's reading from a small, worn book by candlelight, glasses perched on her nose.

Addie and I hesitate, not wanting to interrupt, but she snaps the book shut when she sees us.

"We can come back," Addie says.

"No, please sit. I'm only reading excerpts from the *Tao Te Ching*." We must look blank, because she explains, "It's an ancient Chinese spiritual text laying out the fundamentals of Taoism. I like to be familiar with all of the ancient religions; they hold the ingredients to cleansing and clarifying the soul."

"We hope your stay at Lazy Dog is conducive to your, er, spiritual bath," Addie answers. God bless her; I had no idea what to say myself.

"What can Ms. Jordan and I do for you?" Bianca asks.

"We were hoping to talk with her directly," I say. "We need to tell her about a possible problem."

"She had a headache and is inside resting. She asked me to meet with you in her place."

We sit, and Addie starts. "Okay, well, here's the thing. Have you met the couple staying at the ranch, the Devitas? We think they could be paparazzi." She explains what we've seen.

The psychic rolls her eyes in an uncharacteristic expression of disdain. Usually, no matter what she's saying or doing, she looks as if she's somehow above this mortal plane.

"These people are like the darkness. You may wish they did not exist, but without them, the true and pure light could not be seen."

Uh, okay.

"We aren't sure what to do," Addie says. "They haven't violated any ranch rules, and apparently taking pictures of other people on vacation is rude but not illegal. Still, we thought we'd at least let Kate know our suspicions."

The psychic nods. "Ms. Jordan is grateful for her career and her fans, but there are downsides. The paparazzi are one of them."

"Will you let her know what we told you?" I ask a little impatiently.

"And if there's anything we can do to help?" Addie adds.

"I will." Bianca stands. "Thank you for sharing your suspicions, but I must go. It's time for Ms. Jordan's nightly extermination." From the deep pocket of her sweater, she extracts a small device that I recognize immediately as the electromagnetic field reader we got for Kate. Phil, our handyman, told me it's used for diagnosing problems with electrical wiring.

"Let us know if you find anything." Cheekiness lights Addie's voice. "Pest control comes out monthly, and we like to tell them if there are any specific problems to address."

Bianca shoots her a look and says goodnight.

As Addie and I head up the hill toward home, I say, "Pests? I thought that thing was used to find faulty wiring."

"Cliff says they're also used for detecting ghosts." We both snicker.

"Well, I hope any spooks are off haunting someone else's cabin tonight, so Kate can get some sleep," I say. We won't get that glowing review if she doesn't rest well.

At home, Addie and I let the dogs out, boil some tea —*our* nightly ritual—and head to our rooms.

I sip my warm drink and try to read a few chapters of my book before my eyes slip shut. It feels like only a minute later when Zip, who sleeps on my bed, starts to woof. My eyes open, feeling heavy and itchy. It's eleven o'clock according to my clock. The other two Zs are moving around outside my room. At least, I hope it's the dogs.

Zip jumps off the bed and scratches at my closed door, obviously wanting to get to her brothers, who usually sleep in Addie's room.

I pull on a robe and crack open the door. Down the hall, a lamp shines softly in the living room. Addie's on the couch, her cell phone up to her ear.

"What's going on?" I ask, yawning, as I go in.

She holds up a finger, listening, and then hangs up. "That was the emergency vet in Nederland. Apparently, they had a water leak and are closed for a week for repairs."

"Who's sick?" I look around; the Zs all seem fine. They watch us with curious eyes, tails wagging, probably wondering what fun we have planned for the middle of the night.

"Ace," Addie pulls her robe around her against the night chill as I sit in a chair. "Kate called, asking for the number of an emergency vet."

I smirk. "Was he spooked by the ghosts?"

"Ha - maybe. She said he's acting funny, kind of disoriented. She's worried. I said I'd reach out to the vet. Should we take him to Boulder maybe?"

"Or Estes Park. Why don't we call Travis?"

"He's not an emergency vet—"

"But he said we could call in an emergency if we need to."

Addie shrugs. "Worth a try." She finds his number. It must ring a few times before he picks up.

"Dr. Travis? It's Addie Miller. I'm so sorry to bother you in the middle of the night, but we have a sick dog up here." She pauses. "No the Zs are fine. It's Ace, a miniature doxie who came with a VIP guest." She tells him what she knows about Ace's condition. "Could you possibly talk to the owner and see what you think?" She listens again. "Are you sure?" Another pause. "You're wonderful—thank you so much. One of us will meet you in the parking lot."

She hangs up. "What a nice guy. He and Amelia are driving up. He said they could get here as quickly as we could get Ace to Boulder to be seen."

"That's really kind of him."

Travis is a great guy. He lost his grandmother, Jo, who helped him start his mobile vet business and was his first assistant, just before the first Love & Pets Party last August, a fun community event Travis organizes to provide free and discounted veterinary services and immunizations. From what he told us, Amelia, his new assistant and now girlfriend, came into his life just at the right time both professionally and personally. Addie and I brought the Zs to the party last year to help support Travis, but we missed it this summer. We've been too busy.

Addie curls her legs up on the seat and yawns. "I'll call Kate back and take her and Ace to meet Travis when he gets here. Can you cover for me in the morning so I can catch a little more sleep after?"

"Of course. Thanks, Addie. Sleep as long as you need to."

I climb back in bed and call the Zs. They squirm and snuggle into the blankets until I'm forced into a mere few inches of mattress real estate.

I toss and turn, hoping Ace will be okay. If something happens to him here, not only will I feel terrible, but also that elusive positive review will vanish like the ghosts in Kate's cabin after Bianca puts them to rest.

Chapter Seventeen

❦

Tobias

A new, eye-catching vehicle sits in the staff lot when I pull in—a turquoise RV with the logo Love & Pets Mobile Animal Clinic on the side.

"What now?" I mutter as I climb out of my truck.

I drop my phone in the dirt and curse. Tyler didn't have a good night; I was up a few times with him. Dad's taking him to the doctor this morning, and I know from experience I won't be able to eat or drink much until I hear from them. I wish I could take him, but this week isn't a good time to miss work.

As I tramp past the RV, the door swings open and a guy steps out. He's in his late twenties with dark hair, wearing rumpled scrubs, and carrying a medical bag.

I nod to him. "Morning."

He squints in the newborn sun and looks me up and down. "Are you the new head wrangler?"

I stop and hold out my hand. "Tobias Coleman."

"I'm Travis Brewer. Friendly neighborhood mobile veterinarian."

I jerk my thumb at the RV. "That's some rig you have there. How does she do on the mountain passes?"

He sets the bag down and ties his long hair into a clump behind his neck. "Let's just say she won't win any races in Monaco."

"Did something happen to the dogs?" I wouldn't doubt it. There are more things on this ranch that can hurt a dog than hairs in a horse's mane.

"Not the Zs. A guest's dog is sick."

So, Ace. "What happened?"

"He got into something that made him sick. I induced vomiting, administered an IV, and gave him some meds for his elevated heart rate."

I shake my head. "That's what you get mixing lap dogs with a ranch."

He hesitates and then smiles at me. "Maybe, but . . . doxies are tougher than they look." He tilts his head toward the ranch. "Mind if I join you? I'm going back to check on him."

"Sure, but I'm headed for the barn."

"That's where he is."

A sick dog in my barn? We just got on top of the strangles. I sigh. No use getting mad. Kate does what she wants around here.

As we walk through the hushed buildings, Travis tells me how he met Isa and Addie when they lived in Denver. He was the Zs' vet there.

"Between you and me," he says, "when they told me their plan to buy a dude ranch, I thought they'd be back within a year. But now I'm not so sure. Addie and Isa have put their hearts and souls into this place. They might be unconventional ranch owners, but who am I to judge that? My office is a candy-colored RV."

I chuckle as I slide open the barn door. "It takes more than caring to make a place like this work."

"True. Like experienced people who want to help make it a success as much as Isa and Addie do."

Was that directed at me? Maybe, but he's not looking at me now. I follow him down to the stalls at the other end.

"How's he doing?" Travis says when he reaches the last enclosure, one that's usually kept empty.

"Better I think," Kate says from inside. She's curled up in a blanket with Ace, who's alive if a little disheveled and sad-looking. She sits up, and I see she's wearing thick flannel pajamas and boots with a winter coat. Straw sticks out of her messy hair. Travis kneels down to examine Ace, a stethoscope and light in hand.

"I'm sorry I broke the rules again, Tobias," Kate says. "When Ace got sick last night, I brought him here. The barn has good energy. And down here I could change out the straw and keep him comfortable."

Energy again. What does that even mean? But I tell her it's okay. She could have let him make a mess in her room knowing someone else would clean it up later. And I have to give it to the woman: she loves her animal.

"Good morning, everyone." Isa and a blonde woman in scrubs that I don't recognize come our way from the entrance. The barn is officially becoming a circus. Or a mobile vet clinic.

Isa greets me coolly. "Looks like you've met our Dr. Travis. This is Amelia, his assistant."

Although it must have been a long night, Isa looks as bright as a fresh cut bouquet of flowers. I have trouble tearing my eyes away from her, but I manage to say hello to the woman.

"Thank you so much for letting me use the guest room, Isa," Amelia says to Isa. "The passenger seat in the Love & Pets mobile isn't very comfortable for sleeping."

"Don't mention it. We're so grateful you both came to take care of Ace. How's he doing?"

Kate and Travis have been consulting while we talked.

"He's improving," Travis said. "Looks like we're getting the toxin flushed out. I want to stay a little longer and keep an eye on him. Can Amelia and I bring him to the RV with us for a while, Kate?"

She nods. "I'll go get dressed and meet you there."

I let out a silent sigh of relief. Wayne and Amanda should be here soon, and we have work to do to get the horses ready for the day. I need my barn back.

I touch Kate's arm. "Glad he's all right."

The actress stops and rests her head on my shoulder for a second. Caught off guard, I stiffen. Especially since Isa is watching, a small frown on her face. Isn't playing nice with Kate what she wanted me to do? As Kate, Travis, and Amelia leave, I get Isa's attention.

"Can I talk to you for a minute?"

She looks outside as if she'd like to say she has somewhere to be, but then she nods. "Look, I'm sorry they were in here, but I didn't know Kate would sleep in the barn with Ace until Bianca told us just now. I—"

I lift a hand to stop the flow of words. "I wasn't going to complain about that."

Her mouth shuts, but her eyebrow rises. "Then what were you going to complain about?"

I stare at the ceiling, calling up as much patience as I can muster. "Can we agree to take a break from the sarcasm?"

She looks like she wants to argue, but she nods.

I take a step closer. "The other day at the campfire, what I wanted to tell you before Kate called me over was that I couldn't accept your apology until I apologized." I pause. "I didn't get a chance to do it."

She blinks. "Oh."

"I'm sorry we got off on the wrong foot, Isa. That was at least half my fault."

"Only half?" She composes her face. "Sorry, no sarcasm."

I feel damned awkward, but I press on. "I'll admit I was skeptical about this place when I started, but I'm enjoying my job, and I appreciate the work. So . . . I hope we're even with apologies and we can move on now."

She smiles, just a little lift of the lips. "I hope we can, too."

"See? We can do it," I say.

"Do what?"

"Have a civil conversation."

"Maybe, but let's not push our luck," she jokes.

I grin. "Have a nice day, Isa."

She gives me a long, searching look that elevates my heart rate. "You, too, Tobias."

I do my best not to watch as she walks away.

Chapter Eighteen

Isabel

"I wish he wasn't coming," I say for the third time. And for the third time, Addie nods. This time she sighs, too.

It's Friday, our one night off a week, and we're driving the ranch Jeep to the Lonely Buck Bar for Cory's charity event.

"I know we're friends now and everything." I wave a hand. "But he makes me uncomfortable. He's so judgy."

"And you aren't?" she says.

"Tobias deserves to be judged!"

"Isa, did you know you have a tendency to hold a grudge?"

"I'm Italian. Of course, I do!"

Addie laughs and pushes her Ray-Bans up her nose. The radio's playing classic rock. I don't know any of the songs—this music is way before our time—but Cory will be playing it, so we're cramming.

"You know, you might give the guy a little bit of a break," Addie says. "Have you heard about his son?"

Son? Tobias has a son? "Tobias is *married?*"

"Not as far as I know. But he has a seven-year-old with some health problems."

I sit back in my seat. "Like what?"

"Wanda didn't know the details, but Myra told her that Amanda said that he was talking to a doctor on the phone about his son's treatments for something. Sounded serious."

I watch the yellow and white highway lines slip by as we travel the last couple miles to Estes Park. Tobias is a dad? And his son has medical issues? Guilt burns through me like a shot of tequila.

Addie glances at me. "None of us knew."

I nod, but shame settles into the pit of my stomach nonetheless. Addie parks the Jeep behind the bar. The parking lot is practically full, and music already pours out of the place through the cracks. I lean over to check my hair in the side mirror as I get out.

After a long week, part of me wishes I was on the couch with a bowl of popcorn, a blanket, and the Zs curled around me—my usual night off. But we want to support Wanda, Cory, and the volunteer fire department.

Inside, the place is packed. The Lazy Dog crew is settled at several tables in the back. The college kids—mostly housekeepers and wait staff—sit at two tables, and the permanent staff sits at two more. I search for Tobias. He's with Wanda, Myra, Wayne, and Amanda, laughing at something Cliff said, beer in hand.

Tobias catches me looking, but I'm a little proud that he can't quite tear his eyes away again. I'm wearing a black sweater, skinny jeans, and my dressy pair of cowboy boots. I used the flat iron on my hair and spent extra time on my makeup. When I smile, he smiles back.

The chair next to him is empty.

Screwing up my courage, I head toward it. But all five-foot-ten captivating inches of Kate Jordan slides in before I can get there. She must have been in the bathroom.

I stay the course and walk to their table to say a brief hello. As I do, I realize practically every eye in the bar is on the movie star. Especially the male ones. Of course. She's wearing a tiny denim jacket and black leather leggings with high-heeled ankle boots. Her golden hair absolutely glows in the shadowy bar.

How did she even find out about Cory's show? Looking at Tobias, I have a good guess. *Move along, Costa.* Addie and I aim for two chairs at the other end of the table, greeting our employees as we go.

Someone hands me a beer poured from a pitcher. I take a sip, but I won't drink much. I'm the designated driver home.

Cory's group, The Hair Band, finishes setting up onstage. He introduces some key members of the fire department, and they thank everyone for being here. Then the band tears into a song that sounds like Led Zeppelin. Then again, Led Zeppelin is almost the only band from this era of music that I know. Now that I think about it, I'm not sure how Cory is such a fan of classic rock. He's not that much older than me.

Addie's chattering away with Dale who scooted down so we could squeeze in. I lean to my other side to hear Wanda and Myra.

"Looks like a great turnout," I half-shout when there's a break in the conversation. "Good work getting the word out, Wanda."

"I won't leave a Facebook post unshared for my aspiring rock star." Wanda puffs her chest out proudly and folds her arms over the top.

As Cory finishes the song and starts another, Myra says, her voice a high squeak, "Did you hear about the cold front coming in?"

"No, when?" I ask.

"The beginning of next week. We're supposed to get snow."

Wanda snorts. "You know those weather people can't forecast their way out of an open box."

"They sounded pretty sure," Myra says.

A commotion at the other end of the table grabs my attention. Tobias is on his feet, a man's arm in his hand. The guy is middle-aged, bearded, and his movements are sluggish. He yanks his arm out of Tobias' hand but steps closer. And hands on hips, all five and a half feet of Cliff back Tobias up.

Kate backs her chair away. Addie and I jump to our feet and walk that way, while off to the side, Laura Devita snaps pictures of the scene.

Tobias speaks to the man. "Hasn't anyone taught you that no means no, man? She told you she didn't want a drink, she doesn't want to dance, and she definitely doesn't want to have your children."

"I know that asshole means asshole," the guy slurs. He pokes a finger at Tobias' chest. "And I know one when I see one."

Tobias smiles. "Yeah, good one. Now, take off before I call the cops."

"I just wanted a dance," the guy mutters before slanting his way across the packed dance floor.

Kate peeps out from under her wispy bangs at Tobias, who's righting an upset beer glass.

"You okay?" he asks her. I can't hear her response, but she doesn't seem hurt.

"What happened?" I ask Cliff.

He shakes his head. "Some people really shouldn't drink. They should get high on music, like me." He swivels his hips.

"What did the guy say?" Addie asks.

"Asked her to dance, but he wouldn't go away when she said no, so he got mouthy, and Big T stepped in."

"Big . . . T?" I say.

"For Tobias. And for throb." Cliff waggles his eyebrows. "As in *heart*throb. I know you ladies were thinking of another kind of throb."

We laugh, but heat crawls across my chest and neck. Tobias did look a lot like a hunky cowboy bodyguard. And the Devitas got pictures. I can practically hear the stalkerazzi still snapping away from across the bar.

"Should we check on her?" Addie asks me.

Kate's clutching Tobias' arm, looking grateful. "She seems fine now."

Addie and I head back to our chairs, and Cliff follows. After a minute or two, Jamie the waitress joins us, sitting beside Addie. Cory's Hair Band isn't bad; I find myself moving to the music, especially the slower songs.

"Cliff, you're a musician?" Jamie asks with a big smile.

His chuckles. "You're just now hearing this?"

"She's new, Cliff. Give her a minute," I say.

"I am a musician. And a performer," he tells her.

"I am, too!" Jamie says. "I mean I sang with an *a capella* group in college, and I had dance training in high school. Where did you train?"

I suppress a smile. I'm sure it was on the dance floors of various clubs back in New York City, where he's from.

"Alvin Ailey," Cliff answers.

Addie and I stare at him.

"You did?" I ask. "How did we not know this?"

He sips his drink. "You didn't ask."

"It's not in your employee file," Addie says.

"Would you include formal dance training on an application to be a housekeeper?" he asks.

"No, but, Cliff—"

He waves a dismissive hand. "It was a long time ago."

"How did you end up out here?" Interest lights Jamie's face.

Cliff sighs and puts a palm over his heart. "A large bottle of tequila, a gambling debt, and a beautiful woman. But that's a story I rarely tell."

Addie and I exchange a wide-eyed glance. From her head-shake, she had no clue, either.

Clearly changing the subject, Cliff asks, "How is Kate's little dog doing?"

"Much better," I say. "Travis and Amelia took good care of him." I pause. Now that Jamie got him talking, maybe he'll tell us more about himself. "Do you have any pets, Cliff?"

"I'm not home enough to take care of one. And I get plenty of time with your weenies." He winks.

A man I don't know walks by. He's dressed up as if he came from a board meeting. He nods to us but stops when he sees Cliff.

"Clifford! I haven't seen you at poker night in a while. How are you?"

Cliff stands up to shake his hand, and the man pulls him to the side to talk.

Addie blinks at me. "Poker night?"

I shake my head. "Cliff is a wild and wonderful mystery."

Jamie moves seats to talk to one of the waiters, while Addie gets drawn into a conversation with Wanda and Myra. As Cory starts a new song, someone takes Jamie's empty seat beside me.

Tobias.

Chapter Nineteen

Isabel

I glance down the table at Kate. "Is everything okay with—"

"She's fine. Talking to Cliff," he says.

I sip my beer to hide my nerves. "I didn't know they'd met."

"I think she went to her room while he was cleaning and heard him singing."

I bang the glass down. "Was he wearing clothes?"

Tobias eyes me with amusement. "As far as I know. Why?"

"No reason." If he hasn't heard about Cliff's propensities to sing half-naked yet, I won't be the one to tell him.

"Anyway, Cliff invited Kate tonight, so he can entertain her for a while."

Cliff invited Kate? That rocks my world for a moment.

Tobias nods at my drink. "I'm going for another pitcher of beer for the table. What are you having?"

"I was planning to get seltzer water." I shrug. "I'm driving."

"Got it."

He squeezes in at the bar and chats with the man and woman sitting beside him as if he's known them all his life. He probably has. I think he said his parents' ranch wasn't far from here.

I have the urge to check my face with my phone camera, an old habit from high school when I had pretty bad acne. I always check to make sure I don't have an angry zit poking through my carefully applied foundation and powder. It mostly cleared up in college, but I still break out under stress, and the urge to check is especially bad when Tobias is around.

I open my wallet as he sets my drink down.

"Relax, Isa, it's just water. I can cover it."

I fidget with the glass, running one finger up and down the cool side as he settles back in his chair. What to talk about? I'm so accustomed to either arguing with him or avoiding him, I'm at a loss.

"Thank you for intervening with that drunk guy," I finally say.

"No problem. Honestly, I'm not sure why Kate goes out in public between the paparazzi and fools like him."

He sounds a little possessive, which makes me feel . . . jealous?

"She has to live her life, I guess," I say.

"Then hire a bodyguard instead of a tea reader. Might be safer."

"Where is Bianca tonight?" I ask.

"Back at the ranch, babysitting Ace."

I snort. "I like the little guy, but I'm not sure you could pay me enough to do her job."

"Me, neither."

Tobias and I smile at each other. We agreed on something! Amazing! Addie's still wrapped up her conversation with Wanda and Myra, so I take a chance and lower my voice.

"Tobias, I just heard you have a son."

He studies my face. "You look shocked. Can't imagine a woman wanting to have a child with me?"

"No, of course not! I mean, of course, I can. Ugh, you know what I mean." I flush. "Anyway. I heard he's seven? What's his name?"

"Tyler. Big T."

I almost choke on my fizzy seltzer, remembering what Cliff called Tobias. Luckily, he doesn't seem to notice.

"What's he up to tonight?" I want to know if the boy's mom is in the picture, and I can't think of another way of asking indirectly.

"With my parents. We're staying with them for now, and they keep him during the day while I work." His pauses. "He has some medical issues."

Tobias' face tightens, making me think there's a lot more to the story. It seems thoughtless to change the subject, but I also don't want to pry by asking what's wrong with his son. I must look as conflicted as I feel.

"Cystic fibrosis." He takes a drink. "Know anything about it?"

I shake my head. He tells me it's a genetic disorder that causes mucus to clog Tyler's lungs and throat. He has daily treatments to keep the airways clear and address breathing problems.

"His mom was a carrier of CF, although she didn't know it because she was adopted. Ellen couldn't really deal with the guilt. She took off a few years ago." He stares at the stage. "Anyway, we almost lost Ty a few times when he was a baby, and he's dealt with the disease ever since."

"How awful." I swallow hard. "Tobias, I had no idea."

"I don't talk about it much at work. I try to keep those worlds separate, you know?"

"You don't have to, though. Really."

Addie and I like to think we're building a little family at the Lazy Dog. That in time, our staff's families will be our families. He nods, but . . . after the way I've acted, I wouldn't be at all surprised if Tobias doesn't believe me. Shame gnaws at me again.

"What about you, Isa? Any family? Boyfriends or anything?"

It would secretly be nice if he held his breath, waiting with tense anticipation for my answer, but his voice stays light.

"If you count three delinquent dachshunds." I grimace and cover my face at exactly how lame that sounds, but he only laughs. "No husbands or boyfriends or anything. My family is back in Denver."

"Is that where you grew up?"

"I'm a native. Although my family's originally from Italy by way of New Jersey. My parents moved to Colorado for an adventure, and they fell in love with the state."

I tell him about them, Luca and Angela, a scientist and realtor, and my grandmother, who watched Emilio and me for years after school.

"Nonna taught me to bake like a *panettiera* and curse like a sailor."

"Sounds like a well-rounded education."

I laugh. "It was."

"And now I know where you get your fire from."

I raise an eyebrow, but he says it with respect. "My sass, at least."

I'm sitting close, mostly so I can hear him, but also because he's very easy to be near. His voice is mellow, his eyes twinkle when he's amused, and he smells of leather, like a worn-in, comfy chair. I want to curl up on his lap with a blanket.

"Tell me about your parents," I say.

"Dad's a third-generation cattle rancher, and Mom's a homemaker. My sister Tamara teaches fourth-graders out in Grand Junction. She's married with two boys a few years older than Ty."

"I'd love to meet Tyler sometime." I sort of blurt it out, and then regret it.

I really do want our staff to be like family, but as I hear more about Tobias' life and share more about my own, I wonder if I should maintain some distance. He's an employee, after all; I need to be careful not to cross lines with him or any other staff.

"I'd like that, too. And my folks would like to meet you; they've heard a lot about you."

I make a face at him. "I'll bet they have."

He grins. "They don't have much choice. I'm home most nights with Ty."

"You sound like a good dad." A few weeks ago, I wouldn't have believed it, but now it doesn't seem surprising at all.

"I do my best. He's a great kid. He deserves everything I can give him, for as long as I can give it." A cloud passes over his face.

I touch his arm. "Tobias, cystic fibrosis isn't . . . I mean, he won't . . ."

He runs a hand through his hair and swallows. "The average life expectancy is going up all the time."

"Let me know if there's anything you need," I say. "Time off for his appointments, a few more nights a month to get home early—"

"I can manage." His voice is steely.

I pull back; I must have gone too far.

After a second, his shoulders slump. "I'm sorry I snapped. I don't like feeling pitied."

I meet his eyes. "I'm not pitying you. I'm offering support. As your employer and as I hope, a friend."

His jaw tightens, but he nods. "Thanks. Really. I appreciate that."

Cory and his band finish a raucous version of *American Woman*, a song I actually know, and he thanks the crowd for coming to support the fire department.

"Because of you, we raised ten thousand dollars!"

I clap with the crowd, and Tobias puts his fingers to his mouth and whistles, something I've never been able to do.

"For a finale," Cory says, "I'd like to welcome a very talented performer to the stage. He's the man behind the popular Disco Divo YouTube channel and a star of the four-star Lazy Dog

Ranch up off the Peak-to-Peak Highway. Y'all welcome Cliff King to the stage."

Applause and cheers erupt, and not just from the staff tables. People all over the bar yell Cliff's name and hoot. I shake my head. How does everybody know him?

Cliff takes the stage, talks to the band for a moment, and then launches into a strutting rendition of *We Are Family*. I've heard Cliff sing before. But on stage, with lights, an audience, and a live band to back him up, he takes his performance to another level.

People had been moving off the dance floor as Cory's band finished, but they fill it again when Cliff gets going. Amanda and Wayne head out there, and Addie goes out with Wanda, Myra, and Jamie.

Although I've only had a few sips of my beer, liquid courage fills me. I take a settling breath and glance at Tobias.

"Want to dance?"

He smiles, but before he can say what I hope is *yes*, Kate grabs his bicep. She's already moving to the beat.

"Let's dance!"

He hesitates, his eyes on me. With a sigh, I tilt my head toward the dance floor. Looking not entirely happy, he follows Kate to the floor. As they move together, the Devitas aren't the only ones snapping pictures.

My heart hammers and I berate myself. Did I really ask Tobias to dance? What was I thinking? I *just* warned myself to have good boundaries. Of course, now he's dancing with stunning Kate Jordan instead. Yes, he's doing exactly what Addie and I told him to do and taking care of our VIP guest.

But as I watch her gyrate against his long, firm body, her arms over his shoulders and face tipped up to him, singing the lyrics, I wonder for a moment how much care he's taking of her.

Not fair, Isa. And none of your business.

Addie waves to me to come out. With a smile that's only a tiny bit forced, I do, turning my back to Tobias and Kate.

At least he and I have come to an understanding. Maybe even laid the foundation for a friendship.

And considering where we started, I'd call that excellent progress.

Chapter Twenty

Tobias

On Tuesday before the morning ride, Wayne comes to the stall where I'm grooming Apple. The mare never gives me any trouble; she's a laid-back girl who likes her spa treatments.

"Weather is calling for snow," he says.

"Yeah, I heard." Snow happens in the mountains, even in September. I brush Apple a little extra under her neck, where I know she likes it. "The first flakes aren't supposed to come until early morning, but I'll take another look at the reports."

I mean to check the weather at lunch, but I'm distracted by talking with guests and then the arrival of Kate, who always demands my attention—in the most undemanding way. By focusing all her attention on me, she forces me to focus back on her. I should've eaten in the barn like I sometimes do when I need to get work done on my break.

"Did you see the headlines this morning?" Kate asks. I shake my head. I've learned that she loves—or hates—politics. She gets all worked up about it, anyway. I don't have much time for the news.

"I can't believe Congress is letting him get away with this," she says. "Of course, they've let him get away with everything *else*, so . . ."

She's usually happy to talk, and I'm okay with listening. In that, we're pretty compatible. I don't think we have much in common otherwise, but she doesn't seem to care. As she fumes about the latest objectionable tweet, Isa enters the dining room through the kitchen door. She lifts her chin at me in greeting before stopping to chat with a guest. The woman never seems to rest, which makes me admire her work ethic and worry about her health.

She's in her usual ranch wear today, but my mind wanders back to the vision of her gorgeous curves in that fitted black sweater, jeans, and boots at the bar the other night. Her hair was loose, begging to have hands running through it, and—

Kate touches my bicep, something she seems to like doing given how often I find her hand there. "Tobias? Did you hear me?"

"Sorry, no."

"I'm thinking about coming on the afternoon trail ride." She pats her mouth with a napkin. "Aren't you leading it?"

"Yes, ma'am." Amanda's off this afternoon.

"Great. We haven't gotten to ride together." She pulls out her phone. "I'll tell Axel to book it."

She'd learned the rules quickly after she got here. If you want to ride, you have to book it in our system. But I laugh. "Can't you book it yourself?"

"That's what I pay him for." She smiles at me. A genuine smile—not a smirk or a sneer.

And that's the curiosity of Kate Jordan. Although she's obviously rich and pampered, she's also surprisingly straightforward. She sees her assistant as providing a service—one she's probably paying a small fortune for—so she's using that service. It's a simple equation for her.

I get the sense she actually likes Bianca and Axel a lot, but if they quit tomorrow, she'd wish them well and start looking for a new entourage. Don't ask why she seems to favor spending time with me. Of course, she's easy on the eyes, so it's not exactly a hardship. But while I'm welcoming, I don't encourage her. And I don't have much to say.

I don't know. The woman is a puzzle.

When she finally loses steam, I take my chance to escape. "I'll see you this afternoon for the ride. Dress warmly; temperatures are dropping."

I make my way over to Isa, but I don't interrupt her conversation with the guest. I don't mind waiting—and watching—as she talks. I'm getting to know her facial expressions pretty well by now.

She has one smile that's clearly her *I'm listening, but only to be polite* smile. She uses this one with the college students when they're complaining about their jobs or their hours. I don't often see it when she's talking to guests, but occasionally it comes out when a guest goes on and on about something, like those tiresome Hamiltons from Florida, and she has somewhere else to be.

She has the *I'm genuinely interested* smile, which she uses with most guests, or whenever Addie or Cliff are around.

Then she has her *I'm smiling, but I'm about to call you a nasty name in Italian* smile. So far, that one's been reserved entirely for me.

The smile I love best, though, is her full-on, face splitting, teeth showing beams that I've only seen once or twice. I'd give a lot to get one of those all to myself.

She excuses herself from her conversation with the guest and comes my way. "What's up?"

"Snow is coming," I say. "A couple feet."

"What do you think?"

"We can get the afternoon trail ride in, but the morning ride should probably be canceled."

She nods. "I'll let the guests know."

My lips twitch. "You don't want to check the report yourself? Maybe call the National Weather Service for a second opinion?"

I'm teasing and she knows it, but her lips pinch. "Actually, no. I trust my head wrangler to make the right decisions to keep our guests, staff, and herd safe."

She says this so sincerely; the smile falls off my face. "Thanks, boss. I appreciate that."

She blinks. "Don't, um, don't call me that, please. Isa is fine."

Why not? She is my boss. Could it be because thinking of me as her employee bothers her? I can only hope.

I head back to the barn, still dreaming up scenarios that might conjure Isa's special smile. Scenes that mostly involve us, alone, with a sunset behind us, a horse or two grazing nearby, and my body and lips pressed against hers.

I know it won't ever happen, but a man can dream.

The afternoon trail ride starts out well. Thanks to the cold, only five guests join in. Kate, Bianca, and the Butlers: a dad, mom, and teen son from Seattle who thankfully have riding experience.

Within thirty minutes of setting out down the trail, though, I wonder if I made a bad call. The horses were less than enthusiastic about getting tacked up for the ride, for one thing, and I respect their opinions. It's even colder than I expected, for another. The frosty air paralyzes my nose and crackles in my lungs when I breathe. We're losing the sun, and my riders aren't dressed for much colder temperatures than this.

I probably should have turned around ten minutes ago, but

Kate was riding beside me, talking and distracting me. I grab the horn and twist in my saddle to face the group.

"The weather's turning faster than I'd like. We should probably head back early."

Normally, the ride is an hour and a half, but with the look of those clouds thundering in from the northwest, the light will fade soon. Simplicity, the gelding I'm riding, nickers nervously. I pat his neck.

As we start back for the barn, I realize I'm more right than I want to be. The clouds loom overhead, and within minutes, open up. Snow drives at us in sheets instead of flakes, and the temperature falls with it. I've rarely seen a storm hit so fast and hard.

"Sorry folks," I raise my voice to be heard over the whipping wind. "We need to move quicker, but I'll keep us at a safe pace."

Wayne chose the horses today. Being new, I'm not sure which of them are comfortable on snowy trails. At least the riders don't seem too worried—yet. Everyone's starting to shiver, though. They blow on their hands, and their faces turn pink.

I should have canceled the ride. *Bad decision, Coleman.* But all I can do now is get them back quickly and safely.

We're picking our way through the building snow on the ground when Sagebrush, Kate's horse, stops. I pull up next to her and urge the mare on with a click of my tongue and a tug on the bridle. She won't move. Her eye rolls back at me, and she shuffles her hooves anxiously.

I dismount and try leading her, Simplicity's reins in my other hand, but Sage won't budge. She sticks close to my gelding, squashing Kate's leg in the meantime, and actively resists any attempts to move forward.

The others wait for us, but everyone looks ready to get back to the barn. I have to make a decision.

"Bianca." She's the most confident and calm rider of the group. "I'll have to lead these horses back. I want you to guide the others to the barn. I'll call Wayne to meet you as quick as he can, and don't worry if you lose the trail, the horses know the way."

This plan isn't ideal, but it'll have to do.

Bianca looks at Kate with obvious worry. "Do you want to ride with me?"

"Go ahead, B," Kate says. "I'm fine with Tobias."

The group starts off at a quick walk. Azure, Bianca's horse, looks unfazed by the snow, and the other horses follow readily. I call back to the barn on my walkie-talkie. "Wayne? You still around?"

I tap the device with cold fingers, waiting. A crackle, and then my wrangler's nasally voice comes through. "Yeah, unfortunately. You guys okay out there?"

I explain the situation. "I need you to saddle up and meet the rest of the group."

"I'll be on the trail in five minutes."

I thank him, grateful he has a good head on his shoulders. I've worked with worse. "Better let Isa or Addie know, too."

"How about you? Are you all right?" I ask Kate, who's huddled in her form-fitting coat.

"Just a little cold."

"Let's get you back then."

I lead Sage and Simplicity down the trail, Jack Frost nipping at my nose. That Christmas song is quaint until you feel it in real life. Nips become nibbles and then full-on, painful bites.

"What film are you making next?" I ask.

"It's a remake of *Blue Velvet*. Have you seen the original?"

I shake my head. "I like movies, but I don't have much time to watch them. And I usually go for the action-adventure kind." I lower my voice like I'm telling a secret. "I'm kind of a sucker for westerns, too."

She laughs, a tinkling sound like sleigh bells, and then blows on her fingers. "You're so refreshing, Tobias. Most of the people around me can't wait to tell me about all the films they've seen, and especially mine. They rush to assure me how *original* or *spec-*

tacular my performances are. Have you ever even seen one of my films?"

I scrunch my numb nose. "That one where you were a dancer. I forgot what it's called."

She laughs again. "*City of Dreams.*"

"Yep, that was the one." My walkie-talkie squawks and Isa's voice comes through. "Tobias?"

I steel myself to be yelled at—and rightly so. "I'm here."

"Are you and Kate all right?"

"A little cold but hanging in there." I wink at Kate, although I'm cursing myself inside. I'm sure Isa wants to chew my butt for not canceling the ride.

"Wayne's on his way to meet the group. I have the Jeep; can I drive out and pick up Kate?"

I look at the actress, who nods sheepishly.

"Sounds good. We're on the Sunset Trail, probably a quarter-mile from the access road. Can you meet us there? And bring a blanket?"

"I'll be there."

Relief washes through me. Wayne will make sure the group gets back safely. Isa will get Kate to her cabin before she freezes solid, and I can get Sage and Simplicity to the barn for a good rub down. If it's a wet, cold, and miserable walk, well then, I deserve it.

The Jeep and especially its driver are welcome sights. Isa's covered head to toe in a knee-length puffy coat, beanie, and gloves. She rushes out of the vehicle with a hat and blanket for Kate.

"Addie's bringing hot tea to your cabin, too."

Kate accepts the blanket. "Thank you, but I'm fine. Really. Tobias took good care of me."

Isa glances at me. I almost wince, expecting to see the flash that means she's unhappy with me. Instead, I see . . . amusement? She reaches into the car.

"I brought you a hat and gloves I fished out of the lost and found." She hands them to me, a smirk in her eyes.

The gloves are fine; they're the neoprene type people use for skiing. But the hat is a knit one a kid might wear: brown and white with a horse's eyes and nostrils stitched on the front, ears on top, and a yarn tail. I grimace but yank it gratefully onto my cold, snow-covered head.

Kate grins, and Isa's smirk remains firmly planted on her lips as they slide into the vehicle.

"Call if you need me to come back for you." Isa waves out the window before rolling it up.

My cheeks a little warmer now, I jam my cowboy hat over the cap and lead the horses on through the snow.

Chapter Twenty-One

Isabel

We're lucky to get Kate, Bianca, Tobias, and the Butler family safely back once the snow starts, because the storm quickly becomes a blizzard. The forecast had called for a foot of snow over two days. We get a foot in the first five hours.

The storm's strength takes all of us, including the weather people, by surprise. As good as they are at predicting the weather with models, data, and modern equipment, Mother Nature still has a few tricks up her sleeve.

Luckily for Addie and me, most of the staff is still on property as the drifts pile up. Phil uses his monster truck to shuttle a handful of the local people home that can't leave young children by themselves, but the rest choose to stay and help out. Many of the college kids have trickled back to school, so their rooms are open to house the refugee staff.

We have enough provisions, and Wanda and Myra are here to prepare meals. The guests seem content to sit by the cozy fireplace in the lodge after dinner that night, drinks in hand, while the kids watch a movie in the activity center with the kid wranglers. All is well—at first.

Addie and I visit with guests, the Zs snoozing by the fire, when the lodge's overhead lights flicker, come back on, flicker again, and go out. Like snowstorms, power outages in the mountains during bad weather aren't exactly a random occurrence. I wait for the backup generator to kick on.

When it doesn't, the dogs lift their heads and look around. So do the humans. At least we have the light of the fire to see by. I imagine the frightened whimpers of the kids in the darkened movie room.

"I'll get flashlights," Addie says. "Everyone stay here, please, until I get back."

The backup generator must have failed. And the one staff member that knows how to *fix* the generator is Phil, who went home with a promise to be back with his snowplow attachment in the morning. I curse to myself.

The guests stand, obviously worried about their children.

"My daughter is next door. Where are those flashlights? Don't you have any candles?" Sharon Hamilton's shrill voice rises over the murmurs of others. I grit my teeth. Almost everyone's kids are next door, lady.

"We have several in each building. Addie should be back at any moment with them."

My walkie-talkie makes noise. It's Tobias. "Generator down?"

I walk away from the guests and lower my voice. "It looks that way. And Phil's at home."

"I'm on it."

I gasp. "You can fix a generator?"

He chuckles. "I guess we'll see."

"Okay. Let me know what you find."

Addie distributes flashlights while I call over to the activity center. The kid wrangler answers, sounding harried.

"Is everyone okay over there?" I hear something that sounds like singing, but no screaming, so that's something.

"We're okay. A few of the kids freaked out when the lights went out, and one girl tripped and fell and says her wrist hurts, but Cliff came out of the housekeeping office with a flashlight and started singing to the kids. Some of the kids have cell-phones, so they're using those flashlights, too."

I realize what I'm hearing: a slow, crooning version of *Night Fever*. He's sung that one for me before.

"Please tell me he's fully clothed."

The kid wrangler hesitates. "Mostly."

I shake my head. Cliff is an original. I'm just not sure an original of *what*.

"We'll be over in a minute with their parents. Hang on." I remind the adults about their phone lights and let them know their kids are okay as I leash the dogs.

"Bring people over to the activity center," I tell Addie. "I'll go see if anyone's wandering around outside." The cabins' power will be off, too, so any guests already in their rooms could need help. "Tobias is seeing what he can do with the generator."

Addie nods that she heard me as she hands out the last of the flashlights. I grab a light and pull on my coat. I hate to take the dogs out in the cold, but I can't leave them here alone, either. I shouldn't be out for long.

As we head toward the Kissing Bridge to cross to the cabins, the snow is already up to their low-hanging bellies, and flakes freckle their fur. "Sorry, guys. We'll be quick." They wag their tails, framed by the circle of light around them.

I direct my light toward Kate's cabin, but the dogs stop, their heads turned toward the barn. After a second, they yip and pull on the leashes in that direction.

"No, guys! We need to go this way!"

They whine and pull again. I shine the light in the direction the dogs are straining. With the darkness and snow, I can't see or hear anything, but they clearly do. And whatever it is has them excited. Could something be wrong with the horses?

I head in that direction, my feet already icy, and try to reach

Tobias on the walkie-talkie. There's no answer. I call Addie and tell her where I'm going.

I find the path down to the barn, and the dogs and my light lead me down it. The broadside of the barn comes into view.

The few horses in the stables nicker as the dogs and I go in. Most of the herd will weather the storm out in the pastures. I walk past the stalls, swinging the flashlight back and forth to check each horse, and then take a second to blow on my hands to warm them. Nothing seems amiss in here.

Outside again, the Zs pull me toward the equipment shed beyond the barn. And that's when I remember. The tractor—and the generators—is out here under an open carport attached to the shed.

The dogs strain harder as we approach. Finally, I see why they wanted me to follow them. Next to the generator, Tobias lies unmoving on the snow-dusted ground.

Chapter Twenty-Two

❧

Isabel

He groans as I kneel beside him. His pale face is cold to my touch. The dogs bark, wag their tails furiously, and lick his bare hands.

"Tobias, can you hear me?"

His eyes flutter open and, after a second, focus on me. He tries to sit, but I gently press him back.

"Stay still for now." I look him over and then touch a dark spot in his hair. My fingers come away crimson. "The top of your head is bleeding."

"Stupid," he says.

I blink. "What?"

"Me. I kicked my screwdriver under the tractor, crawled under to get it, and hit my head crawling back out."

"I'll get the first-aid kit from the barn." I run, the Zs racing ahead of me, and return as quickly as I can with the kit and a clean towel to stop the bleeding. Tobias is already tinkering with the generator when I get back.

"What are you doing? You should rest," I say. He doesn't respond. "Let me at least try to stop the bleeding. It's dripping on your coat."

He takes the towel and mops his head. "Give me two minutes, I can get this running."

"Tobias—"

He ignores me. Infuriating, exasperating man. I give up and sit on a low wood box a few feet away, the dogs huddled around me. My face is numb, but at least we're out of the snow.

"Why did you come down here?" Tobias asks.

"To find you!" I say.

"But . . . how did you know something was wrong?"

"I didn't, really. The dogs heard you, or heard something, and pulled me this way."

He glances at the Zs, his expression soft, and wipes a trickle of dark blood from his forehead before going back to his work. After about five minutes, he squats behind the generator.

"Cross your fingers," he says.

It kicks on, and around the ranch, lights flare. I crumple with relief.

Tobias gets to his feet but grimaces. "I'd appreciate that first-aid now."

The dogs jump up as I stand. "Okay, but I'm taking you back to my house where I can clean the cut properly with soap and water." I step close to scan his face. He looks pale. "Are you sure you won't pass out or anything?"

He smiles tiredly. "A headache—and my pride—aside, I'm fine."

It's an easier walk back to the house from the barn with the lights on. Lovely, even, with the snow slanting through the pools of light along the path up the hill.

"Is Tyler with your parents?" I ask.

"He is. They're fine, last I heard. Eating popcorn and watching a classic Broncos game. My dad recorded every big game over the last twenty years. Tyler loves watching them with him. Puts Mom and me to sleep, but it's their thing."

I laugh, thinking about how my mom and I used to watch old movies together during the holidays. Our favorites are *Love, Actually* and *A Christmas Story*. The scene where Ralphie accidentally curses while helping his father change the tire on the family car makes us howl with laughter every time.

I settle Tobias in a chair in the kitchen and gather a bowl of soapy water and a few towels while the dogs gather around his feet. Standing behind him, I clean his hair and scalp as best I can before working my way down to the cut. The blood flow has stopped, but his hair is matted, making it slow going.

"Are you sure you're okay?" I ask. He seems extra quiet.

His shoulders bow. "Honestly? No. Today was a disaster."

"It was an accident. We all have them."

"Not that. Well, not only that. I should have canceled the trail ride. I put our guests at risk."

Our guests. As if part of him already feels some ownership and responsibility for this place. Warmth spreads from my hands, where I'm touching his head, to somewhere around my heart.

"I make at least three bad decisions a day," I say. "I appreciate that you're reflecting on your choices, but you can't tell the future. You chose as well as you could with the information you had at the time."

He's quiet again for a minute. "Thanks, Isa, for helping me. I owe the Zs thanks and an apology, too." He leans down to scratch their backs. "I didn't think little dogs like these should be on a working ranch, but they've grown on me." Still behind him, I can't see his face when he pauses, and his voice deepens. "While I'm being honest . . . I was wrong about you and Addie, too. You're doing a good job running this place. You're great with guests, you hire quality staff, and you let us run our areas without micromanaging. I know none of that is easy."

I rest a hand on his shoulder, my eyes suddenly blurred with tears. We don't get many compliments from our employees. Like many supervisors, it's complaints more often than not.

"Thank you," I whisper.

He places a callused hand on mine. His fingers stroke my skin, leaving burning trails. I swallow, trying not to tense or shiver.

I can't do anything that gives away how weak in the knees his touch makes me feel.

Chapter Twenty-Three

❧

Tobias

After Isa patched me up and we had that moment, I slept over.

In her guest room, that is.

She insisted I go straight to bed and rest, although I was feeling fine. Better than fine, really, since I got the chance to touch her. But with the day I'd had, bed was probably where I needed to be.

The next morning, I lie there a few minutes longer than usual, remembering the feel of Isa's hands on me last night . . . and wishing they could be on me again.

More snow is coming down, so no trail rides can go. I'm happy to have a day in the barn with Wayne, taking the time to organize, clean, sort out the tack, and sort out my feelings for my gorgeous, compassionate, fiery, employer.

He tells me tales about his brothers as we work. He comes from a family of six boys. Wayne, his brothers, father, and grand-father are all named Ray, with different middle names.

"So," he says, already laughing, "when our friends would call the house and ask for Ray, my grandmother had to say, 'Okay, but do you want Ray Steven, Ray Malcolm, Ray Wayne, Ray James...' and she'd just keep on going until the person would say 'the one in high school.' And she'd go through the three or four of us still in high school until she narrowed it down."

I laugh as I polish a saddle, making the leather shine, but I wouldn't know what it was like to have a big family or a brother. And at the rate I'm going, Tyler will be a lonely only.

Wayne clears his throat, interrupting my thoughts.

"Uh, boss? Someone to see you."

Kate stands in the barn door. She's bundled in tall boots and a long puffy coat and hat. Her blonde hair shimmers in the late afternoon sun. I smile at her, but inside I sigh. I want to finish up and get home to Tyler to see how his early snow day went. They've plowed the highway by now.

I wipe my hands on a towel. "What can I do for you, Kate?"

"Can I talk to you?" Her blue eyes slide toward Wayne. "In private?"

Wayne waggles his eyebrows at me behind her back and spits tobacco dip juice in a cup. One of the first rules I set when I started this job was making sure Wayne used a spit cup instead of the barn floor.

I grab my coat and Kate and I walk outside. Horses, many of them covered in winter blankets, walk through the sparkling meadow toward the feed we set out for them. It's that time towards the end of a storm when the snow still falls but the sun also peeks through the clouds. Snowsun? Sunsnow? Whatever it's called, it's pretty.

I thrust my hands in my pockets. "Did you survive the storm?"

She nods. "I lost power in my cabin for a while, but Bianca and I lit candles. She was doing my nightly reading."

Whatever that means. I shift my feet and wait for her to say what she came to say.

"I'm leaving tomorrow instead of Saturday. I got an audition I've been wanting."

"Congratulations," I say.

"Being here has been good for me," she says softly, her eyes on the horses. "I needed some downtime. I've been so tired." She pauses. "And I enjoyed my time with you. You're very easy to be around."

"Thank you. You are, too." I'm not lying. Being with Kate is easy. I just listen and nod once in a while.

She smiles at me. "You're so—and I hope you understand I mean this in the best way—simple. Uncomplicated."

Because you don't know me, I want to say, but I hold my tongue. I've held my tongue a lot over the days the actress has been here. I want Kate to sing the praises of the Lazy Dog to her rich, influential friends and devoted fans as much as Isa and Addie do.

"I have an offer," she says. "One I hope you'll agree to."

I stand up straighter and tip my hat back, which makes her smile and wrinkle her nose.

"It's so cute when you do that," she says.

"Do what?" I ask.

"Push your hat off your forehead like that. You do it when you're surprised or thinking or sometimes unhappy."

I'm starting to sweat now despite the cool air. I don't like being under a microscope; I'm not a bug.

"What are you after, Kate?"

She steps closer, turning her body slightly toward mine. "You, Tobias." She peeps up at me. "I'd like to see more of you. Not anything serious; I don't need a commitment. But I'd like to spend time with you." Her fingers hook on my belt at the side of my waist.

"How?" I ask. "Where?"

"Wherever. You can come visit me at home in Los Angeles or on weekends wherever I'm shooting, and I'll come here when I'm free." She pulls her lower lip between her teeth for a second. "I'd pay you, if that makes things easier, with no expectations of anything in return. I wouldn't want spending time with me to be a financial burden for you."

"I have a son—"

"I know, Tyler. And I know you have this job and a life."

I think about that. I have Ty, my folks, and my job, but do I really have a life?

"Think about it, Tobias." She leans in close. Close enough that I can see the specks of green and gold in her light blue eyes. "Think about the possibility of us."

She kisses me. Not a passionate or deep kind of kiss, but a lingering one. When she pulls away, I taste her lip gloss on my lips. She smiles at me, or maybe at the dazed expression that's probably on my face, tugs her hat down over her ears, and walks away through the snow.

I watch the horses in the meadow for a long time, collecting my wits, and then head back into the barn to finish my work.

Chapter Twenty-Four

❦

Isabel

As Kate, Bianca, and a healthy-as-a-tiny-horse-again Ace pull out of the Lazy Dog Ranch parking lot in their Uber Lux on Friday morning, the staff breathes a collective sigh of relief. Except for Tobias, maybe. He spent a lot of time with Kate while she was here. And I sensed something strange between them when she hugged him and said goodbye at the lodge.

Standing together, they made a beautiful couple. I imagine the tall, lean, white gold beauty of any children their genes would create together. Why no, that's not bitterness you hear at all that I practically forced him to spend time with her.

Addie and I held our breath until the very last day of Kate's visit, hoping nothing else would go wrong. She didn't seem too upset about the power outage. In fact, she was fairly easy, as guests go, despite her special diet, her psychic, her tea leaves, and the stalkerazzi. Now, all we can do is pray that she had a good time and hope she'll tell all her friends, fans, and followers.

Please, please tell them.

We spend the weekend in a flurry of activity, seeing the rest of that week's guests off, checking that the cabins are spotless and in good repair, the kitchen freezer and pantry are restocked, and the staffing is at the right level.

I'm sitting with Wanda in the staff room on Sunday after lunch having just gone over the menu for next month. She's complaining about how much her husband Al spent last month on his hobby of collecting vintage firearms when I catch the words *Tobias, Kate,* and *California* all in one sentence.

Amanda's talking to Myra. The wrangler leans in; her sun-lined face is alive with the gossip she's obviously spilling. Nodding at Wanda as if I'm listening, I eavesdrop on the other two.

"So then, Kate told Tobias she wants to see him again," Amanda says, "and that she would *pay* for him to fly to California or meet her some other place."

My chest tightens. Kate asked to see Tobias again?

Myra's black eyes are huge. "And what did he say?"

"I don't know! Wayne got worried they would bust him, so he went back to the tack room."

Myra screeches and cups her cheeks. "No! Men! You couldn't have dragged me away until I heard how he answered."

I'm leaning so far toward their table that I almost fall out of my chair. I right myself and focus on my salad.

"The stupid things don't even work!" Wanda says. I make a sympathetic noise, but my attention flies back to the other table.

"Wow," Myra says after sucking the last of her iced tea through a straw. "I mean, Tobias is a sweet slab of man ham, but this is *Kate Jordan* we're talking about."

Amanda nods. "He'd be crazy not to say yes. Just to get some amazing trips out of it. Think of the places she'd take him."

"Private jets, five-star restaurants," Myra says.

"Probably wild sex, too," Amanda says. "Don't all celebrities have wild sex lives?"

Myra squints doubtfully. "Can you picture Tobias having wild sex?"

They think about it, which forces me to think about it, too. Not that I've ever wondered before what the, er, sweet slab of man ham is like to kiss. Or hold. Or to make love to. Nope, I've never wondered any of that.

Both women nod at the same time. "I can definitely picture it."

My heart sinks. So can I.

"Isa, you okay? You look a million miles away," Wanda says.

I am a million miles away—fantasizing what it might be like to be wrangled by our head wrangler.

"What did Al say then?" I ask Wanda sadly.

She wipes her mouth, leaving a streak of mashed potatoes and gravy on the napkin. "So *then*, after I tell him I'll put cayenne pepper in his underwear again if he buys one more thing, he spends $100 on this old piece of—"

I try to listen. I really do. But I'm having trouble breathing at the thought of Tobias not being around anymore. In a short time, he's not only become part of the fun and funky tapestry that makes up our permanent staff but part of my day-to-day life. And . . . I don't want to lose him.

How did this happen? Not long ago I called him something so bad I wouldn't even repeat it to Nonna.

And now? Now I wish he would stay. That's all. Just stay. That would be enough.

Mostly.

Chapter Twenty-Five

❧❧❧

Tobias

"Have you had enough steak, buddy?" I ask Tyler before taking his half-eaten plate.

He nods and lays his head back against the couch. I put my palm on his forehead. He's not hot. He just looks . . . worn out.

I scrub the after-dinner plates extra hard and chip one of Mom's drinking glasses when I accidentally hit it against the counter while transferring it to the dishwasher.

The new doc has seen Tyler twice in the last week. Dad took him back today after the first round of suggestions wasn't cutting it.

Mom pats my back between drying the pots and pans. "Try not to worry, Toby. Tyler is a strong boy. He'll fight this."

For how long, though? When will his body decide it's had enough and start shutting down? With all the advances in medicine, can't the doctors do any more for my son?

I know that's not entirely fair. His doctors are doing what

they can. But I live with the constant fear that Tyler may not be one of the lucky CF patients who get to live well into adulthood.

I smile grimly at Mom and shoot a glance at the living room. Ty has snuggled his way into Dad's lap on the couch; the Broncos blanket covers both of them now. They're watching Sunday Night Football—Broncos versus the Bears.

A loud cheer comes from the television. Dad groans and throws his blue and orange cap on the ground.

"Damn it, Flacco," he says.

"Damn it, Flacco," Tyler repeats.

"Tyler, I don't want to hear that kind of language from you," I say.

"I hear it from you." A grin lifts my son's pale face.

"Not often. C'mon bud, remember what Miss Morris said last year. Bad language is lazy language." Tyler loved his first-grade teacher. He'd do anything she said.

Mom and I finish up and head back into the living room. I sit next to Tyler while Mom picks up her knitting and settles in the armchair.

My eyes drift closed. After trying to please three mistresses the last two weeks—Isa, Addie, and Kate, not exactly an easy task—I'm exhausted. They stay shut as the game goes into half-time, and a commercial comes on.

"Kate Jordan seems to have a new boyfriend," a female voice says chattily. My eyes pop open. "The question is: who is this captivating cowboy? Find out next time on *Entertainment Tonight*."

Behind the woman are still photographs of Kate kissing me outside of the barn.

Tyler sits up and stares at the screen, then at me. "Dad, was that you? Who were you kissing?"

I groan and cover my face. I didn't even see the Devitas slinking around the barn that day when Kate came to talk to me.

Eyeing me meaningfully, Mom stands. "Time for bed, Tyler."

"But I want to know who Dad was kissing!"

I put a hand on his leg. "It's okay, Mom. Let me explain."

I try to say what happened in terms that a seven-year-old can understand. It's not easy. Even Dad looks confused.

"So, this actress wants you to move to California?" he asks.

Tyler clings to his grandpa, tears in his eyes. "No, Daddy. Please! We can't move again."

I look at him straight. "We're not going anywhere, Ty, I promise."

"But you kissed her. Are you going to marry her? In those fairy tale books Grandma reads me, they kiss and then they get married. That's how it works."

"Not in real life, partner," I say. "I didn't know Kate was planning kiss me. It didn't bother me—"

Dad snorts. "I'll bet it didn't."

I emphasize my next words. "And it didn't mean anything."

"Okay, bedtime Tyler. That's enough about who your Dad's kissing," Mom says.

Dad and I hug Tyler before she takes his hand and leads him upstairs.

"Well, you sure do attract the pretty ones," Dad says.

I guess. Ellen was beautiful, with the same coloring as Kate, but look at how that relationship ended.

"So you're not taking her up on her offer?" Dad asks.

"No. Although . . . she offered to pay me."

My father's eyes widen.

"I know how that sounds," I say, "but she said no strings would be attached. And I'm guessing she'd pay well."

I tap my thigh. Tyler's pulmonology specialist's bills will be due next month, not to mention the medications, the respiratory specialist appointments, and new school supplies and clothes.

"I won't move to California," I say. "But I guess I could visit her. See how it goes."

Even as I say the words, I feel cheap. I don't have feelings for Kate. Not like that. But I don't think she has feelings for me, either. We barely got to know each other over the two weeks she was at the ranch.

"So you *are* thinking about it," my father says.

I sigh, my eyes drifting closed again.

"I don't know, Dad. I don't know."

❧

Later that night, Tyler tugs on my comforter, startling me awake. I shoot up, fighting my way out of covers and unsettled dreams.

"Dad," Tyler's voice is wet, "I . . . can't breathe."

"C'mere, partner." I reach for him. He comes into the circle of my arms. He's cold to the touch.

"Let me get dressed and we'll go to the hospital."

I talk to him, trying not to panic as I pull on jeans and a Broncos sweatshirt Dad left when he cleared his clothes out of the guest room closet. My own skin is clammy, and my heart pounds against my ribs like it's fighting for its life.

I find my car keys and wallet and scoop up Tyler with one arm. He barely weighs anything at all, a thin slice of a kid. He's still in his pajamas, so I grab a jacket for him on the way out, rushing into the cold, dark Colorado night to the car, the ground crunching underfoot.

I'll text my parents from the hospital. No need to wake them only to sit and worry half the night. And I'll email Isa and Addie to let them know I won't make it to work today.

If I'm lucky, this will be a long night in the emergency room followed by at least one day of an inpatient stay with pulmonology consults so Tyler can be stabilized. I'll have to worry about how to pay for it all later. In my experience, insurance doesn't cover anywhere near everything.

And if I'm not lucky?

I can't think about that.

Chapter Twenty-Six

❧

Isabel

"Cliff, are you in here?" I call as I step into the housekeeping office.

"I'm here. And I'm going to—" He sings about lifting me up where I belong.

I frown and rub my aching temples. "I know that one. That's not disco."

Cliff steps out from the laundry room with his arms full of clean, white towels and sets them on a laundry cart full of cleaning supplies.

"I can appreciate a good ballad when I hear one. Plus, I love me some Joe Cocker. If nothing else, he had a real rock star name." He grins cheekily.

I hand him the list of cabins that are occupied with new guests. We only have about half the reservations we had last week. Fewer bookings are to be expected in fall, but the mild nauseated feeling and tightness in my chest won't go away whenever I think of our bottom line.

After looking over the list, he asks, "Did you hear about Kate and T—"

"Yes." That's the other reason I feel sick and tense. I busy myself with pretending to review the housekeeping work schedule on the table.

Cliff lays a gentle hand on my shoulder. "I don't think he'll go."

I turn my head toward him. "You don't? Why? Did you talk to him?"

"No. But there's his boy, for one thing. I get the feeling that kid is the sun to his solar system. And I think he likes his job."

I press a palm to my forehead. "No one is *that* committed to their job."

"You boss ladies are. When's the last time you two had a real break?"

I don't have to think about it. "Not since we bought the ranch."

"See what I mean? And I like to think I've been fairly devoted to this place. Although if I got the chance to go make my music for real, mmm. *On the radio—*" He croons.

"I don't know that one," I say.

"Donna Summers?"

When I shake my head, he squints with disappointment. "I need to make you that playlist I've been promising. Anyway, there's another reason I don't think Tobias will take that offer. He seems to have a special interest in a certain spirited, dark-haired female around here."

My heart stutters, but I joke to cover it. "You mean Nightrider?" Tobias has been working with the mare a lot.

"No, I certainly do not mean a horse. I—"

The housekeeping door bangs opens and Jamie the waitress bursts in. "Cliff, did you see the— Oh, hi, Isa."

Cliff and I stare at the phone screen she's thrusting out. On it is a screenshot of two blond people kissing. By a barn. In the snow. Two very familiar blond people. By a very familiar barn.

I step closer. "Is that——?"

"Yes!" Jamie squeaks. "It's Tobias and Kate Jordan! Those paparazzi people took it. The pictures were on TV last night, along with one of Tobias confronting that guy at the Lonely Buck, the campfire, trail rides, everything! They're calling him her new boyfriend."

Cliff's eyes are on me so I don't react, but my heart feels like it's sliding into a deep, dark hole.

"They make a pretty couple," I say.

Jamie sighs. "More like drop-dead gorgeous."

"I have to check on the kitchen," I say.

As soon as I walk out of the housekeeping office, my eyes find the barn. A few horses are in the paddock, including Nightrider, but no wranglers. I pull out my phone and with a tight chest, check my email. He would tell Addie and me he's leaving in person, right? Not in a text or email? Wouldn't he at least call?

I step into the kitchen, where Wanda's bandaging Myra's hand. I close my eyes, feeling lightheaded. Not today. Please. I can't handle a trip to the urgent care in Estes Park.

"What happened?" I ask.

"Myra got a new tattoo a few days ago. I'm putting a clean bandage on."

My shoulders un-bunch an inch. "I'm glad you're okay, Myra. What's the tattoo of?" It's in the triangular area between Myra's thumb and forefinger.

Myra squints. "Don't laugh, okay?"

"I won't." But who gets a tattoo on their hand that they have to warn people not to laugh at?

Wanda peels back the bandage. The skin under it is red and irritated, but in clear cursive with a few small hearts wound around, is the name, *Cory*.

Myra beams. "He got my name on his hand in the same spot."

I blink. Cory has to be twenty years older than Myra. "I didn't even know you two were dating."

"We've been hanging out for months, but we got together after the charity concert the other night," she says.

The concert . . . a few weeks ago.

"Sometimes love is a slow boil. Other times it burns. Right, my girl?" Wanda pats her assistant.

"Congratulations?" I'm not sure that's the appropriate response, but I feel the need to say something.

Myra thanks me, and then asks shyly, "Did you hear Tobias and Kate were on TV kissing?"

I groan inside. It's only seven in the morning, and I've already heard about it twice. I'd better get used to it; I haven't seen most of the staff yet. Today will not be a good day.

My walkie-talkie squawks. As soon as Addie speaks, I can tell something's wrong.

"Isa, where are you?"

"In the kitchen."

"Come to the office."

I hurry over, banging the door behind me as I go in, which makes the Zs jump up and bark. My headache throbs.

"Is Tobias leaving?" I ask.

Addie's troubled expression grows confused. "Leaving? He said he's not coming in today. Is that what you mean?"

"Not coming in? Did he say why?"

"He had a personal situation come up."

My jaw clenches. "*Very* personal." I pause. "Wait, isn't that why you told me to come over?"

"Because Tobias took a personal day? No, it's this." She points toward an open letter on the desk.

Printed prominently and soberly at the top are a Miami attorney's name and office address. I scan the contents but can't make sense of the words.

"Child endangerment? Poor planning for guest safety? What is this?" I ask.

Addie's blue eyes are glassy. "It's from the Hamiltons' attorney. You know how upset they were about their daughter being injured during the power outage."

"It was a mild wrist sprain!" The girl had panicked when the lights went out, tripped, and fell. "We made sure she was comfortable and offered them a partial refund."

"Well, now they're asking for a full refund. And—they're suing us."

Chapter Twenty-Seven

❦

Isabel

That night, after a lengthy phone call with our attorney, Addie and I sit in our living room watching the six o'clock Denver news, the Zs snuggling with us on the couch. Zip snores in my lap while Zoom kicks his brother in his sleep.

We were too exhausted to do much after dinner except make an appearance at the evening campfire and welcome the new guests to the ranch.

We don't talk about the letter. There isn't much to say. Our attorney told us the "poor planning" claim was bogus. Snow is an act of nature and we had a backup generator that failed. We got it working as quickly as possible. And it wouldn't have been half so quick without Tobias.

The child endangerment claim was more serious. Apparently, we were supposed to be able to anticipate that our backup generator could go out and have emergency lighting in the activity center. Our attorney was less sure we would win that one if the Hamiltons were to push it. She thought we might be better off settling. She's drafting a response.

We feel awful that the Hamiltons' daughter was hurt, but we did everything we could at the time to make sure she would be okay. The thousands of dollars they're asking for in compensation for medical expenses and pain and suffering could be covered by our insurance, but even if it is, it will raise our rates.

And that could kill us. We have such a razor-thin profit margin, I could shave my legs with it.

To make everything worse, I have a sniffle and a swollen feeling in my throat that inevitably means a cold is coming on. I get one every fall when the weather changes, and I walk around like a zombie for a week until it goes away.

Feeling horribly sorry for myself, I scoot forward on the couch. "I'm going to bed."

Addie points to the television, her face slack. I sink back against the cushions. *Entertainment Tonight* just started. On the screen is a still picture of Tobias and Kate.

Kissing.

"That's our barn." Addie gasps. "On TV."

And that's my wrangler. I mean, *our* wrangler.

The show's host—blonde, skinny, and wearing a short dress—sounds delighted to be gossiping about Kate.

"The actress, last seen in the hit film *Slices of Heaven*, in which she plays a waitress who discovers the pie slices she serves her customers contain their destinies in the afterlife, apparently met this as-yet-unnamed wrangler during a two-week vacation at a dude ranch in Colorado. We've reached out to her assistant for more information about their relationship. Stay tuned."

While I try shifting the rock that's suddenly thunked down in my stomach, Addie grabs her phone off the side table and texts furiously.

"What are you doing?" I ask.

"Asking Axel to put in a good word for us when *Entertainment Tonight* contacts him! Maybe they'll mention the ranch by name in their follow-up report. Or better yet, he could suggest they come to do a story about where Kate and Tobias fell in love! They could interview him, us, show shots of the property . . . This could be huge, Isa!"

I close my eyes. When I open them, Addie stares at me with concern.

"What's wrong?" she asks.

"Nothing. I'm fine."

But I can't tear my eyes away from the screen, where the story ends on a lingering shot of Kate leaning on Tobias' shoulder at the campfire. He's looking down at her face. It's a perfect, intimate moment. I have to give it to the Devitas. They do good work.

"They make a pretty couple, don't they?" My voice shakes. Only a little, but a little is all my friend needs.

Addie scoots Zap over, sits beside me, and takes my hand. "Isa, what is it? Are you crying?"

I blink back the tears. "No."

She puts her arm around me. "What's up?"

"He's going to leave us," I say. "We finally have a decent wrangler, and he's going to fly off with Kate to California and leave us."

"Are you talking about the rumors Amanda is spreading? That cowgirl needs to learn to keep her lasso to herself. No one's heard that from Tobias."

"But he took the day off," I say. "Maybe he's already out there."

"Well, if he is, then hopefully he can persuade Kate to tell all her fans about the ranch. We'd have to hire a new wrangler, but that's not the end of the world." She studies my face and her forehead wrinkles. "But . . . that's not what this is about, is it?"

I play with Zip's soft, leathery ear. Her eyes crack open and then fall closed again with a snore.

"Isa," Addie says, "I've known you a long time. I know how you like your coffee. I know you're a really bad dancer. I know what movie you watch when you're PMS-ing." I nod, and we say *The Notebook* at the same time. "And—I know when you're falling for someone. You have feelings for Tobias, don't you?"

I want to protest . . . but I can't lie to my best friend. I cover my eyes. "Yes."

"When did this happen?" she asks. "Last I heard you were ready to run him over with the Jeep."

I shrug and wipe a tear off my cheek. "I was. But then he changed."

"No, he didn't. He's exactly the same as the first time he walked into the barn."

I love Addie, but sometimes she's a little too literal.

"Okay, then, maybe I changed. Or how I perceived him changed, sometime between seeing how he handles both horses and guests with care, watching him tell off the drunk guy at the bar, hearing about all he's done for his son Tyler, and patching up his head during the snowstorm. He has really great hair." I shrug sadly. "But it's too late. He's fallen for Kate. And he probably hates me. Understandably."

"Isa, how could anyone hate you?"

I hold up a hand and count off my fingers. "Caleb from college, Beau from the rec center, Leticia from marketing, Vela from sales—"

"Caleb didn't hate you. He was mad that you didn't want to date him. And Vela was jealous that your numbers were better than hers."

"Your numbers were better than hers, too, but she liked you." Addie doesn't have an answer for that. "Anyway, I know Tobias isn't interested in me. But I wish he'd have the guts to tell us if he's planning to ride off into the West Coast sunset with our VIP guest."

"You don't know that's where he is."

"If you were him, wouldn't that be where *you* were?"

She hugs me. "Oh Isa, I'm so sorry I didn't notice sooner how you felt about him."

"I didn't even know myself until I heard Kate asked him to visit."

"I should have known this was coming."

I make a face. "How?"

"Because you've always hated guys before you fell in love with them. It's your love life MO."

My laugh is a little choked with tears. "That's not true."

It's her turn to count on her fingers. "Kamal in college, who you almost kicked in the crotch before you realized he was only trying to open the dorm door for you, not grab you from behind. Then there was Miguel from Austin, who you thought was trying to have you fired when really he was just trying to find out if you had a boyfriend." She thinks. "Oh! And let's not forget August, your latest and greatest, who you wouldn't speak to for at least a month after he told you he liked your outfit because you thought he could be trying to sexually harass you."

"And now I want to harass Tobias!" I pause. "Wait, that doesn't sound right. I don't want to harass him. I just . . . I like him."

Zip rolls on her back so I can scratch her tummy.

"I'm a wreck, Addie. I haven't been able to think about anything else since I heard Amanda's rumor. Even the lawsuit didn't hit me the way this did."

My friend squeezes my hand.

"I know we can't have a relationship the way things are now," I say. "He's our employee. But I thought Tobias and I would have more time to get to know each other. Time to work together to make the ranch great. I know it's a major switch, given how we started, but I thought we could be friends."

The truth is, I thought there could be something more between us, even if we never acted on it.

And now I *know* that there is.

It's the eccentric, beautiful, and talented actress, Kate Jordan.

Chapter Twenty-Eight

❦

Isabel

Out again today, the text that Addie and I get two days later says. But no word when Tobias will be back.

I pop into the stables first thing, where Amanda and Wayne groom horses for the morning ride. They look up expectantly as I come in, but I only shake my head. No Tobias.

"You two doing okay? Do you need anything?" I ask.

"Yeah," Wayne grumbles, "another pair of hands."

Amanda shoots him a look. "He'll be back soon. Give the guy a break."

"He's taking a break all right. A long one. In Kate Jordan's bed."

I wince but cover it by smoothing a lock of hair out of my face. "I'm sorry about this. We've asked Tobias to tell us when he'll be back, but he only says he's not sure."

Which is maddening. And so far, other than the general locale of Colorado, Entertainment Tonight hasn't said where Kate vacationed when she met her hunky cowboy. So our booking volume hasn't even benefited from the Kate and Tobias story. Not that I really want it to. The whole thing makes my stomach ache. Along with a runny nose and a cough, I'm pretty much miserable.

Amanda pats Apple's rump. "We can handle things, Isa. We did before Tobias came, and we will again if he doesn't come back. Right, Wayne?"

Wayne grunts. I wonder again why Amanda didn't want the head wrangler job. Gossip aside, she would be good at it, but she turned Addie down when she approached her about it over the summer.

I walk from the stables up to the housekeeping office. The sun is late getting out of bed. The mornings have turned cold and crisp, requiring a winter coat, hat, and gloves whenever I'm outside.

Winter is coming. And without Tobias, without any kind of promotion after Kate's visit, and with the Hamilton lawsuit bearing down on us, the Lazy Dog Ranch might not survive it. At least, not with its current owners.

Addie and I need to have a serious talk about how long we can make this work. We've pretty much used up our savings, and we have business loans that I don't want to think about. We have a five-year plan, but we didn't meet our first-year sales goals. We're off track for year two as well. The five-year plan looks less attainable every day.

I try to remember that many, many new ventures fail. Lots of BHAGs don't work out the way they're planned. It happens. But it hurts.

I rub that painful spot on my chest that won't seem to go away and scrounge in my pocket for a tissue to wipe my nose. Tobias leaving brings up equal parts sadness, hurt, and anger.

I know, I know. I have zero right to be angry with him. A famous actress took a liking to him and offered him the deal of a lifetime. Talk about BHAGs.

But if Kate Jordan had never brought her dachshund,

psychic, and skinny little yoga tights to the Lazy Dog, Tobias would be in the barn right now, not off in Hollywood.

I shake my head. Time to focus on things here and now, things that I can actually control. Like our serious shortage of housekeepers now that the college kids have left for school.

"Cliff?" I call as I step into the office.

He twirls toward me, a white towel secured with clothespins around his waist. It's I Will Survive this morning. Seriously, the man has an uncanny ability to pick the right songs at the right moments.

He sashays, throws his arm in the air for the finale, and smiles at me. "Good morning, Isabel."

"Is it?" I sink into a metal folding chair that has worn linens needing to be recycled hanging over the back. "I hadn't noticed."

Cliff unclips the clothespins and whips the towel off with a flourish. Even after all this time, I'm still tempted to look away, just in case. But, as always, his shorts are underneath. Still breathing hard from dancing, he perches next to me in another chair.

"I'm glad you're here. I know you're having a hard week."

I glance at him and nod. "I am. Thanks for noticing, Cliff. I'm—"

He holds up a hand to stop me, his expression sympathetic. "And I'm about to make it harder."

My stomach clenches. Not more bad news. "What is it?"

"I'm leaving Lazy Dog Ranch."

I reach for his hand, my thoughts spinning. "Why? Have we done something? You know we can't offer you more money, but . . . how about more time off to work on your music? Maybe we could do that."

He grins again. "See, that's the thing. I'm about to be able to make music full-time."

"What? How?"

"Well. After Kate saw my performance, both at the Lonely Buck and the more, er, impromptu variety, she wanted to see more. I sent her the link to Disco Divo, she followed me, liked a few songs, told her followers, and overnight," he twirls his free hand around, "I've got producers wanting to work with me. More than one. I told you disco is coming back."

"You did." Tears fill my eyes as I hug him. "I'm so happy for you, Cliff." Except, I can't believe this. First Kate took Tobias. Now Cliff?

"I told them I'd fly out for a meeting next week, but I won't quit until you find someone to take my place. I won't leave you and Addie between that nasty rock and a hard place."

I thank him, but I doubt we'll ever find someone capable of taking Cliff's place. He's truly one of a kind.

❧

I tell Addie about Cliff's opportunity at lunch. It's hard not to feel like the ranch is a slowly sinking ship that our staff is jumping off of by the day.

She chews the inside of her mouth. "This is bad, Isa."

I nod and put a forkful of food in my mouth, barely tasting the delicious brisket that Wanda and Myra made.

"I'll spend some time posting his job," I say. "And I'll follow up with a few applicants for the rest of the open housekeeping positions. Have you heard anything new from Tobias?"

We have his job description all worked out, of course, but the last thing I want to do is use it.

"No, but I did hear something about him." Addie lowers her voice. "Jamie the kid wrangler's boyfriend slammed his finger in a car door. She took him to the hospital, and she said she saw Tobias there. She didn't talk to him because he looked like he was upset. She didn't think he saw her."

My heart pirouettes. Could he be at the hospital instead of with Kate? Wait, if he's at the hospital, did that mean something happened with Tyler? Or maybe one of his parents?

I tap my nails on the table. "Do you think I should check on him? Or would that be inappropriate since he didn't tell us this himself?"

"It's been three days. I think it would be nice to check on him, especially after hearing this. I can give him a call since you're busy working on hiring."

"No, I will," I say quickly.

Addie smirks and gathers our dishes to take to the kitchen. "Let me know what you find out."

My palms sweat and my arms itch thinking about talking to Tobias, but I have to do this. I have to find out once and for all if he's leaving.

Chapter Twenty-Nine

❦

Isabel

Tobias' address, filched from his employee file, is a ranch road between the Lazy Dog and Estes Park. It's a beautiful drive north along the Peak-to-Peak Highway.

Normally, I wouldn't dream of stopping by an employee's home unannounced. But I tried calling him all afternoon and it went straight to voicemail. I'm really concerned now. So I jumped in my car.

I hope he doesn't report me to the chief human resources officer. Wait, I *am* the chief human resources officer. Anyway, I'm praying he understands my visit comes from a place of concern and not a place of, like, stalking.

I park in front of his parents' home. It's a simple ranch house with a barn and extensive pastures beyond. The only sign of Tyler, or any children, is a partially deflated football on the porch and a dusty bike that looks like it hasn't been ridden since Tobias was a kid.

I ring the doorbell, my knees shaking and heart quaking.

How will he react? An older woman with gray-blonde hair and kind blue eyes shaped like Tobias' eyes opens the door. She wipes her hands on an apron and smiles at me.

"Hello," she says. "Can I help you?"

I love how much more trusting people are in the mountains. In Denver, she'd be eyeing me through a peephole and yelling through the door.

"Yes, um, hi. I'm Isabel Costa. I'm looking for Tobias Coleman." I stutter when I'm nervous, which I absolutely detest. And what's with the formal names? Am I serving a warrant or something? My smile falters.

"Isabel? Are you the new owner of the Lazy Dog Ranch?"

"Yes, that's right."

"Isa!" She reaches for my hand. "Oh, how kind of you to stop by. I'm Tobias' mother, Katherine. Please come in." I step into the entrance, and she leads the way to the sunny yellow kitchen in the back. The views from the house are as stunning as at the Lazy Dog.

"You must have heard about Tyler," Katherine says. "Toby is at the hospital with him. I'm making some dinner for when my husband gets back. Toby will eat with Tyler and spend the night, but Billy comes home for dinner. You know hospital food."

Relief courses through me, although I instantly feel guilty that it does. Tobias isn't in California. He's with Tyler at the hospital. Why didn't he just tell us that?

"I'm so sorry, Katherine. Will Tyler be okay?"

Katherine glances at a picture on a small built-in desk of a very thin young boy with blond hair, blue eyes, and only a hint of a smile. It could be Tobias as a child if it weren't for the modern clothing.

"He needed more intensive treatments than usual, but he's recovering. They're releasing him tomorrow, we think. Toby's been there night and day, and Billy and I have taken turns visiting and holding down the fort here."

"This is Tyler?" I touch the picture.

Katherine nods with worry in her eyes. She points to another, more faded photo beside it. "This is Toby at the same age."

Toby. Tobias doesn't seem like the type to have a nickname, somehow. Maybe because his more formal name fits him so well.

"They're handsome boys, aren't they?" she asks.

I meet her smile. "They are."

She moves to the kitchen counter where raw chicken parts perch on a cutting board and dough is half-rolled out on another surface. The oven preheats.

"I'm sorry I interrupted you," I say. "I'll go. I'll touch base with Tobias tomorrow after Tyler is released."

She frowns. "No, no. Stay for a while. I can use the distraction."

"How about if I help then?" I walk to the sink to wash my hands. Katherine protests, but I ignore her. "As my dad says, if you've got time to lean, you've got time to clean. Or help make dinner."

"I wish my Billy would take that to heart, especially when the Broncos are playing. Or when they're interviewing the coach. Or when there's news of a trade or a player injury." She laughs.

"He's a Broncos fan?" A glance into the living room answers my question. It's neat and cozy but littered with Bronco paraphernalia: blue and orange blankets, a baseball hat, a stuffed horse wearing a jersey, and a branded drinking cup on the table. I remember Tobias told me his father and Tyler enjoyed watching games together.

"Oh, yes, and Tyler, too. He wants to have a Broncos-themed birthday party when he turns eight in a few weeks."

"What about Tobias?" I ask. "He's not a football fan?"

"Tobias did 4-H, riding, and rodeo instead of football . . . much to his father's disappointment. Toby was a good athlete, but he had no interest in team sports."

"Lucky for us that he stuck with horses."

I'm secretly glad that Tobias isn't football crazy. Emilio has a friend on the Broncos' staff, so I've been to a few games, but I'm not that into the sport.

Katherine trims and breads the chicken while I roll out the dough and cut biscuits. We work in silence for a few minutes.

"I'll bet you're glad to have Tobias and Tyler back in Colorado," I say.

"I am. They've had a hard time the last few years since Toby's ex-wife Ellen left."

Tobias didn't say much about his ex when we talked about Tyler at the Lonely Buck. I don't want to pry, but my curiosity flares.

"Ellen was a good girl," Katherine says, "but she couldn't handle the guilt or responsibility of Tyler's illness. Not only were they facing a serious disease for their son, they knew they wouldn't be able to have other children. It was too much for her to handle."

"I'm sorry. What a difficult situation."

"It was. And is." Katherine doesn't sound angry with her former daughter-in-law, only sad, so I hold back on saying what I'd like to about a mother who leaves her sick child. I wish compassion came a little easier for me.

"Tobias is lucky to have you and Billy for support," I say.

She smiles. "And he always will have us."

I slide the biscuits into the oven while Katherine slips chicken into the fryer.

"What else can I do?" I ask.

"Stay for dinner with Billy with me. The least we can do is offer you a meal for stopping by to check on Toby *and* making the biscuits."

"That's very kind, but I should be getting back to the ranch. Will you please let Tobias know we're all thinking about him and Tyler?"

Or we will be, now that we know what's going on. Why didn't he confide in me? Then again, why would he, given how we started out? He told me he keeps his work and personal lives separate. But come on, this is different. Or it should be.

"Tell him to take all the time he needs," I add.

"I know he'll appreciate that, but he'll be back to work as soon as Tyler's home. He's a hard worker, my Toby."

"And we've missed his hard work since he's been away. We've missed him." I'm embarrassed by how plaintive I sound.

Katherine's blue eyes twinkle as she opens the door for me. I get the sense she could tell I meant more than I said. Suddenly, I wonder what she knows about Tobias and Kate Jordan. If only I could ask her . . . but I draw the line at interrogating an employee's mother. Instead, I hug her.

"I'll say a prayer for Tyler."

"Thank you." Her eyes shine. "We need all the prayers we can get around here. I'm so grateful to know Tobias has such a kind and understanding employer."

Employer. The word blares in my head like an alarm as I drive back to the ranch. Will Tobias see my visit as kind and understand or as meddling? Is it meddling?

I'm very glad to know about Tyler being hospitalized. Addie and I will help Tobias and his family however we can, but I need to keep the boundaries between he and I very clear. I'm his employer, and he's my employee.

No matter what my personal feelings are, as it stands now, that's all we can be.

Chapter Thirty

❦

Tobias

The day I get back to work after Tyler's discharged, I go looking for Isa.

My heart and brain have wrangled since I heard she came to my parents' house and—helped my mother with dinner?

Shock, bewilderment, and hope swirl around inside me. I don't know what brought Isa there, but I'm burning to find out. My mother only said she came to check on me.

I rub my tired eyes as I search the ranch for her. It's been a long few days. These hospitalizations take a lot out of all of us. The toll it takes on my parents is visible in the dark circles under their eyes, not to mention my frail boy.

I search the ranch from the business office to the dining room and lodge and then check the housekeeping office. Please don't let this be one of Isa's rare mornings off. If I have to, I'll go knock on her door up at the main house, like she did mine.

"Hey, Cliff," I say as I enter. "Have you seen—?"

I stop. One of the other housekeepers is in Cliff's usual spot.

"Hi, um," I scramble to think of her name, "Marisol. Where's Cliff?"

"Haven't you heard? He's in California meeting music producers."

"What? When did this happen?"

"While you were out." The older woman's expression turns sly. "We all thought you might see him there since Kate Jordan helped Cliff meet the music people."

"You thought I might run into Cliff in . . . California?"

"Yes, when you were there with Kate."

I take off my hat and scratch my scalp. I didn't get enough sleep for this conversation. "Let me get this straight. You think I was in California with Kate for the last few days?" I laugh; it was such a far cry from the truth.

It's Marisol's turn to be mystified. "Not just me. Everyone thinks that."

Everyone. Which means Isa, too. "Have you seen Isa? I need to talk to her."

The housekeeper smiles knowingly. "Handing in your resignation, huh? Remember us when you're rich and famous, Tobias."

I walk out, breathing deeply to clear my head. This day is already going downhill. Isa must have thought I was in California with Kate until my mother told her otherwise. That changes things.

I'd hoped Isa came to check on us out of concern. That her heart might be softening toward me. Now I'm not so sure.

I also realize I should've shot straight with her and Addie about why I was out. I'm so used to keeping my personal life personal, and it honestly didn't occur to me that she, or anyone, would think I followed Kate to California at the first crook of her finger.

I keep searching and finally find Isa in the barn of all places, along with Addie and Wayne. Isa greets me but looks away quickly.

"Tobias—you're back. I'm so glad." Worry clouds Addie's face.

"Is there a problem?" I ask.

"It's the Zs," she says apologetically. "They took off after a family of whitetails, and they haven't come back."

"When was this?"

"About half an hour ago. They're usually gone ten minutes at most," Addie answers.

"We were asking Wayne if he'd seen or heard them. But don't worry, we'll find them ourselves," Isa says quickly.

She sounds ashamed about the dogs going AWOL. She probably thinks I'll yell at her.

"Is Amanda coming in today?" I ask Wayne.

"Every day, since you were out," he says with a pointed look before spitting in his dip cup.

I deserve that, too. I owe my wranglers an explanation and a lot of gratitude for covering for me.

"Can you hold down the fort for another hour while I help them round up the dogs?" I ask Wayne.

"You don't need to do that," Isa says.

I look at her square. "I'd like to help. Please. And Nightrider probably needs the exercise."

A search and rescue mission with Isa seems like the perfect time to talk this out. If I can help find the Zs at the same time, even better.

She hesitates as if trying to decide if what I'm saying is what I mean. She does that a lot. One of these days, I'll tell her that the upside of my personality is that I almost always say what I mean, or I don't say anything at all.

"Thank you," Isa says quietly. "I'll take Apple. Addie, could you be ready with the Jeep in case we need help?"

The women share a look, and Addie nods. Wayne watches with plenty of interest. I'll bet the gossip machine's been running at full capacity since the *Entertainment Tonight* story broke.

Isa and I tack and mount the horses and guide them out of the paddock. "Which way did they go?" I ask.

She points north, down one of our lesser-used trails. We set off that way, scanning the hills and the surrounding brush, calling the dogs' names.

I'm watching for them, but it's hard to take my eyes off of Isa. With the denim stretched over her long legs and the cold air reddening her cheeks and making her dark eyes shine, she's radiant.

I try to think of something neutral to say before questioning her about why she came to my parents' house. She beats me to it.

"How's Tyler?" she asks. "Is he home from the hospital?"

I'm surprised, not by what she asked, but by how worried she sounds. I know by now that she's a more compassionate woman than I initially gave her credit for, but I still find myself bracing for a fight when we talk.

"He's better. Home, resting, and his breathing is clearer than it has been in months. We have his new pulmonologist's attention now, which is sometimes half the battle."

She smiles, clearly relieved. "That's wonderful news, but . . . I wish you'd just told us what was happening. Addie and I thought you— Well, we didn't know what was going on with Tyler, so we couldn't support you. You don't have to do this on your own, Tobias."

I swallow hard against the lump her words bring to my throat. I've done everything on my own until a few months ago. Accepting my parents' help was damned hard, much less other people.

"I'm sorry," I say. "You're right. I should have told you." I glance at her. "My mom liked you, by the way. She said you were 'as sweet as Halloween candy'." I imitate my mother's voice. "Dad said you make a mean biscuit. Tyler and I snagged a few when we got home. They were delicious."

She laughs, which lifts my spirits a few inches. "Your mom was really kind to me, especially after I barged in like that."

"So . . . you came to check on us?" I ask.

"Yes," she says. "What did you think I came to do?"

"Fire me," I joke. "I'd been gone a while."

Her body stiffens. "I would never come to your *home* to do that."

I curse myself. Here we go again.

She's stone silent for a few seconds, and then she grins. "I'd wait until you were in my office where I could really let you have it. And slam the door on your way out."

I chuckle. I'd heard Isa had a sense of humor, but she'd rarely shared it with me before.

The trail has been quiet, only the wind and a few hawk calls. So my ears perk when a dog barks in the distance.

"Hear that?" I say.

Isa nods, and we nudge the horses to move faster. Nightrider tosses her mane nervously. I pat her neck and murmur to her.

The sharp barks come from our right, down a hill that ends in a gully. We can't take the horses off-trail safely—too steep and too many rocks.

"Can you take Apple?" Isa asks. "I'll go see what's going on."

I climb off and hold both horses' reins. "Be careful."

Isa picks her way down the hill until I can't see her. After a minute, there are several loud, shrill barks and then whines.

"Everything okay?" I yell. There's no answer. I'm about to tie up the horses and climb down myself when I see the top of her head.

She's carrying one of the dachshunds, and the other two follow close on her heels, their low-slung bodies barely clearing the sharp rocks.

"It's Zoom," she says. "I think his leg might be broken."

The poor guy is whimpering, and his front right limb doesn't look right.

"I need to carry him, but I don't think I can ride one-handed," she says. "I might lose control of Apple or drop Zoom."

"I can." I pass her Apple's reins and climb on Nightrider.

Looking relieved, she lifts the dog up to me; he licks my hand weakly.

"I'll tell Addie to call the emergency vet and let them know she'll be bringing him in. I don't think we can wait for Travis, even if he had time to come up."

"Got it. Ride safe back." Holding Zoom firmly, I turn the mare toward the ranch.

I may not be the knight rescuing the princess—more like the stable boy rescuing the princess' dachshund—but, hey.

I'll take what I can get.

Chapter Thirty-One

Isabel

By the time Tobias got back to the barn with Zoom, Addie was there with the Jeep. Wayne said she wrapped Zoom in a blanket and immediately took off for the emergency vet. Hopefully, they can set his leg and relieve his pain quickly.

I kept a close eye on Zip and Zap as I rode Apple back. I gave her to Wayne for a quick rub down and comforted the dogs for a minute. They're tired, dirty, and a little lost without their brother. "He'll be okay, guys."

But . . . I can't help thinking again that Tobias might have been right about the Zs. They do cause their fair share of trouble. On the other hand, what's the Lazy Dog Ranch without dogs? As I lead Zip and Zap to the office, there's an unexpected bounce in my step. I'm relieved we found them, but that's not precisely the reason for my good mood.

I didn't dare ask Tobias if he'd made a decision about leaving us, but the fact that he's back, and he hasn't resigned yet, seems like a good sign. On the other hand, he didn't have time thanks to Z's. I won't press him; he has enough on his mind with Tyler. Still, the suspense is awful.

Seated at my desk, I try to get to work massaging the budget for next month and avoiding the even more important work to be done.

After a while, I run out of other things to do and open my email program. I need to give some kind of reply to our attorney's drafted response to the Hamiltons.

Addie and I talked about this, and I've been thinking about it for days. With a settling breath, I put my hands on the keyboard and type.

We won't settle. We believe we did everything we could to mitigate a bad situation, including getting the power back on as quickly as possible and caring for the Hamiltons' daughter.

If they'd come to us directly with their additional complaints, we would have loved to give them a chance to visit us again at a discount or offered them an additional refund. But that clearly wouldn't be enough for these people.

We might end up paying more in legal fees if they take us to court, but not giving in to a petty lawsuit feels like the right thing to do. But I'm sweating as I hit send.

I turn in my swivel chair to stare out the small office window. The view from the Lazy Dog Ranch doesn't look so good. Even if Tobias stays, reservations are down, we're losing staff, and our savings are dwindling.

Our Big Hairy Audacious Goal is getting uglier and hairier by the minute.

I can't think about closing up shop, laying off all the employees who rely on us and who I've come to love, and leaving this beautiful, peaceful place.

But we might have to.

The mountains are hard to see through the clouds today. If the Hamiltons don't drop their suit, and if reservations don't pick up in the next few weeks, the dream Addie and I have worked so hard to achieve will die.

And there's really nothing else we can do about it.

Chapter Thirty-Two

❧

Tobias

Later that day, as I'm closing up the barn for the night, Isa walks in. She's a vision, silhouetted in the barn door, the mellow yellow of the setting sun for a backdrop. My eyes trace her body before leaping guiltily back to her face.

Focus, Tobias.

"Hey. I have an idea." She sounds tentative.

I brush the dust off my hands. "What's that?"

"Your mom mentioned that Tyler's having a birthday soon, and he wants a Broncos party. Why don't we have it here? He can invite his friends, and we can use the dining room, maybe between lunch and dinner? Wanda and Myra already agreed to make the cake and food, Addie and I will decorate, and you can take the kids for a trail ride."

My mouth hangs open for a second. "Really? You'd want to do that?"

She looks hurt, and I kick myself for saying that out loud.

"I already spoke to Addie. We'd love to host it."

I push my hat back, my throat tight. My boy's never had a party.

"That's a very generous offer, Isa, and I know he'd love it. What can I do?"

"Just find a date that works. Addie and I love party planning. Leave it all to us."

Still a little stunned, I thank her again and then ask about Zoom.

"He's exhausted, snoozing by the fireplace with Addie last time I saw, but he'll be fine. The vet set his leg, and we made an appointment with Travis to remove the cast in a few weeks. We were lucky to find Zoom when we did though. He isn't a spring chicken. None of the Zs are."

I laugh. "Could have fooled me when I first met them."

She wrinkles her nose. "I'm still humiliated by the memory of your interview. The dogs, the poop. I can't believe you took the job after all that."

She slumps on a stool, her legs stretched in front of her. I'm tempted to step behind her and massage her shoulders. Tempted, but not brave—or stupid—enough to try it. I sit on another stool to squash my body's reaction to the idea.

As I find myself leaning closer anyway to get a whiff of Isa's scent, like smoke and roses, I have the overwhelming urge to tell her exactly what I'm thinking, how I'm feeling.

I've had a few dates since Ellen left, but I haven't felt anything like this for a woman in years. Partly due to Tyler and partly due to a bruised and broken heart. But that same heart is pumping pretty true right now, and it's getting hard not to let that show.

Except—I have no idea how Isa feels about me. She's been a lot more pleasant lately, and it was kind of her to check on me when Tyler was sick, but pleasant and kind is a long way from the feelings *I'm* having about my employer.

An employer who I'm pretty sure is far too principled to have a relationship with an employee like me.

My cell phone rings. Grateful for the distraction, I pull it out. No name, but under the number it says Hollywood, California. It's not hard to guess who's calling.

She jumps to her feet. "I'll let you get that."

"Isa, wait, I want to talk to you."

Within seconds, she's gone. My jaw clenches as I answer the call.

"Tobias? It's Kate."

Her airy voice is familiar, and yet it already feels like part of the past. I knew the woman for less than two weeks if you can call a handful of encounters knowing someone. She was mysterious and intriguing, but I don't need mystery and intrigue in my life. I have a son with a chronic illness. That's enough uncertainty for one man.

We catch up for a minute, and I ask about Bianca, but after that, I don't know what to say. I guess that's why she invited me to visit her—so we could get to know each other.

"Have you thought more about coming for a visit?" she asks.

"I have. And as flattering as your offer is, I don't think I can take you up on it."

Tyler's hospital stay was a dose of reality. My place is here, with him. Not in California or wherever else Kate goes in the world, no more than some Rocky Mountain man-candy.

There's a pause. "You're welcome to bring your son, of course. I'd like to get to know him, too. I have a pool at my place and a huge game room that only my nieces and nephews use. He'd love it."

I picture Ty and me horsing around in the pool or playing foosball or something. Actually, I can see that fine. I just don't know where Kate fits in the picture.

I laugh lightly. "The stalkerazzi would have a field day with that."

"Oh, the Devitas won't be a problem. I only pay them to take the pictures I want them to publish."

I freeze, and not from the cold in the barn. "Wait, you . . . paid them to take those pictures?"

She laughs, a breathy, sexy sound. "Of course. I thought Bianca explained that to Isa and Addie. My fans want to see me in my *real* life, but I need privacy. So I let the Devitas take and sell pictures that I'm willing to have shared, and it makes my fans happy to think that they're unscripted."

Understanding flows over me slowly, like the dawn. Or maybe the sunset. My voice sharpens. "So, let me get this straight. You wanted people to see us together? You kissed me so they could publish a picture of us?"

"No, Tobias, it wasn't like that. I wouldn't have invited you out here if that was all it was."

I don't know. Maybe that's exactly what happened. Sure, Kate might like me a little bit, but from what Mom told me after watching recent episodes of *Entertainment Tonight*, those pictures the Devitas took started up a firestorm of curiosity from fans and publicity for Kate. More pictures of us together in California couldn't hurt if publicity is what she's really after.

I walk to the barn doors, breathing in the cold air. I'm not angry. If anything, I feel like the trail ahead is clearer than it's been in years. I laugh and run a hand through my hair.

"Listen, Kate, I enjoyed getting to know you, but I don't think I'm cut out for your world," I say sincerely. "And I'm happy here at the Lazy Dog."

There's another pause. "I'm sorry to hear that, Tobias. But I understand. If you change your mind, you can always reach out."

"Thanks. I appreciate that."

I'm about to say goodbye when an idea comes to me. A good one. And after pretty much using me for her own purposes, the woman owes me.

"Hey," I say, "can I ask you for a favor?"

Chapter Thirty-Three

❦

Isabel

I smooth the last Broncos tablecloth over a table in the dining room and then turn to survey my work. I've got blue and orange balloons, plates, and napkins, an old championship game playing on a TV in the corner for the parents, and a Broncos flag on the wall that Tyler can take silly pictures in front of with his friends.

Tobias is at the stables leading the kids' ride with Amanda right now. They should be here soon.

I step into the kitchen. "All set?"

"I think so," Myra says. "We've got Bronco burgers, Thunder fries, and the cake is frosted and decorated. Oops!" As she turns to gesture toward the cake, she flings the pointy cake server at my head. I duck just in time.

Coming in from the pantry, Wanda shakes her head at her assistant. "Myra, I don't know what I'm going to do with you."

I pick up the utensil and hand it to Myra to wash off. "I expect we'll keep her. I already increased our insurance after the

Hamilton girl was hurt. Seriously, though, thank you both for doing this for Tyler."

"Happy to. Any son of Tobias is a son of mine," Wanda says.

"Why do you say that?"

"He got Kate to post that picture the paparazzi took at Cory's charity show to her Instafacechat thingy—"

"Instagram," Myra tells me, rolling her eyes.

"Like I said, she posted to her Snapgrambook," Wanda winks at me, "and said what a good show it was and asked her fans to donate to the fire department. Cory said they don't even know what to do with all the money they got. Although I'm sure they'll find something to spend it on before too long."

"Huh. That was really kind." I'm impressed that Kate was thoughtful enough to ask her fans to donate. And she helped Cliff out. As far as I know, she still hasn't mentioned the ranch in any public places, but I have to admit she's been good to our staff.

As for Tobias asking her to post that, I'm not so sure. Most of the staff still assumes that he was in California with her, and I haven't corrected them because 1) Tyler's health really isn't our business, and 2) as much as I hate to think about it, Tobias still might decide to go. I haven't had time to speak to him in any depth since our conversation in the barn a week ago when he got her call.

Right now, I'm focusing on throwing a fun party for the kids. I pat my jeans pocket to be sure my gift to Tyler is still there.

A few minutes later, Addie arrives with Zip and Zap on their leashes and Zoom in a deep basket she carries him around in. He has trouble walking with the cast, and she can't bear to leave him behind.

"Oh, Isa," she says, "it looks so cute in here! Tyler will love it. This is really sweet of you to do for him and Tobias. If only everyone knew what a wonderful person you are. But if they did, they'd try to steal you to be their best friend, so I won't advertise it."

"Never gonna happen." I hug her. "Oh, here come Tobias' parents. Let me introduce you."

A stream of excited second graders cuts short our chat with Katherine and Bill. There are four boys and two girls, and they all look pink-cheeked and smiley after the ride. The Zs whine, hop up and down and tug on their leashes to greet them, which brings on fresh squeals from the kids. One girl settles down next to Zoom's basket to pet him.

Tobias meets my eye as he comes in, and for a moment, it's just us. Ugh. I have to remind myself constantly that he's an employee. There can't be anything between us other than friendship. But when I see him cleaned up and looking sharp in fresh jeans and a plaid shirt, his hair combed, it's ridiculously hard to remember.

Tobias comes to my side and calls Tyler, who's wearing a Broncos jersey, over. Seeing his son beside him is like looking at the wrangler in miniature. Tyler has a bit darker hair, and a bit greener eyes, but otherwise there's no mistaking Tobias' child. He kneels next to his son.

"Ty, this is Ms. Isa and Ms. Addie, the women who're hosting your party for you. What do you say?"

Tyler's eyes are wide and excited as he takes in the decorations, the food that his friends are digging in to, and especially the massive cake Wanda's carrying out. Good decision not to let Myra do that.

"Thank you very much. It's lit!"

Addie and I laugh, but Tobias scoffs. "Too many sports talk shows with his grandpa."

"Tyler," I say, "I know you want to join your friends, but I have something for you." I dig his gift out of my pocket and hand it to him.

His pale, thin face breaks into an astonished grin at the four glossy strips of paper in his hand. "Broncos tickets? To a real game?"

"A real game. They're playing the Titans in a couple of weeks. I thought you could take your dad and grandparents with you."

"Wow, thanks!" Tyler clutches the tickets like if he loosens his grip, they might disappear. He spares a grin for me before running to show his buddies. "Hey you guys, look what I got!"

Addie pats my arm with a soft smile. "I'll go meet the kids' parents."

Tobias hasn't stopped staring at me. I turn to him and cross my arms to hide my shaking hands. I'm not sure how he'll react to my gift.

"Isa, that . . . that's incredibly generous of you. Too generous. How did you get tickets?"

I lift a shoulder. "I called in a favor from Emilio, and he called in a favor from his friend who works for the Broncos."

His eyebrows pinch together. "It's too much, we can't repay you."

I blink. "It's a gift, Tobias. You don't need to repay me."

He clears his throat and steps closer. His eyes burn with something I haven't seen in a long time. Could it be . . . desire?

"Can I convince you to come with us? Mom would love a Sunday off from football, and I'd . . . I'd love for you to get to know Tyler better. And vice versa."

I shouldn't. I know I shouldn't. But I step a little closer and smooth my voice. "You want me to get close to Tyler?"

He scratches his neck, which is turning a sweet pink color. "If I'm honest . . . I want you to get close to me."

I let my smile take its time coming. "Tobias, you're stammering."

"I'm nervous."

"Why?" I lean in even closer, my eyes on his mouth. He licks his lips, and something inside me jumps.

"Because . . . because I'm falling for you, Isabel Costa. Hard."

My body screams to put my arms around him and tell him I feel the same way, but alarms blare in my head. With effort, I step back.

"We can't . . . we can't do this, Tobias. You work for me. This is wrong."

The partygoers sit at the tables eating and talking. No one seems to be paying attention. Well, Katherine glances our way, smiles, and turns back to Tyler, who's jamming half a ketchup-covered hamburger into his mouth.

Tobias moves in again. He's so close, I feel his body heat. "Then I quit. Effective immediately."

"No! We need you here."

His eyes keep mine. "We? Not you?"

His lips are inches away. What am I doing? Am I about to kiss him right here in front of our staff, guests, and his parents? I breathe in Tobias' scent of leather and fresh hay.

"Isa! Addie! Come here. You won't believe this!"

I blink, feeling dizzy as I turn from Tobias. Myra has her phone in hand, and Amanda holds a half-eaten piece of cake on a plate. The party kids don't notice the outburst, but the parents stare. Addie follows the women over to Tobias and me, looking as confused as I feel.

"Look! It finally happened!" Myra shows Tobias, Addie, and me her phone. Kate Jordan's Instagram account shows a gorgeous shot of Ace standing on a yoga mat, the sun rising above him. And the location tagged is Lazy Dog Ranch.

One of my hands flies to my mouth while the other searches for Addie's arm.

"Hey, that's the rock I told her to do her yoga on. I didn't know she did it," Tobias says.

"And she posted a lot more pictures of the ranch," Amanda says. "A few with you, Tobias." She raises an eyebrow at him. Myra flips through to one of Tobias' triangular back and shoulders as he's leading a ride.

"She raves about her stay." Myra points to the caption. "She says everyone should think about vacationing here."

I can barely read Kate's words through tears of relief and joy. This is what we've worked so hard for. I thread my fingers together with Addie's.

My friend's voice is wobbly as she asks, "I wonder why she posted this all of sudden?"

Blinking away tears, I glance at Tobias. He doesn't look as clueless as the rest of us.

Addie's phone rings, and I glance at the screen as she picks it up. It's a call forwarded from the reservation line, something we do if the front desk is on a break. She answers with the smooth sales voice she perfected years ago.

"Thank you for calling Lazy Dog Ranch. How can I assist you?" She pauses. "A reservation for November? Of course. Give me just a moment to pull up my booking calendar."

Addie grins at me and waves her arms around over her head, phone in hand, as she heads for the business office. The dogs watch her go but stay behind to scavenge scraps off the ground under the tables.

As Myra and Amanda high five each other, Myra drops her phone. "Well, crap. That's another crack in the screen."

"Can I speak to you in private please?" I ask Tobias and walk outside without waiting for an answer.

When we're far enough away that no one can see us from the lodge or dining room, I face him. "Tobias, why did Kate post that now?"

He shrugs and shifts his feet. "She had a good time, I guess."

My eyes narrow. "Did you have something to do with it?"

He brushes the backs of his fingers along my cheek and jokes, "The good time? Or her post?"

I scowl and move away from his hand. "The post."

"That depends."

"On what?"

"On whether you'll be angry if I say yes."

I sigh. "Tobias, I need to know, once and for all, if you're taking Kate up on her offer."

He looks baffled. "What? No. Wasn't that obvious?"

I make a frustrated noise. "No! I've been on pins and needles wanting to know. It's been the only gossip around here for weeks!"

He shakes his head, his eyes pinning mine. "I'm not going to Hollywood or anywhere else."

"But why not?" I ask. "Kate has everything. She's gorgeous, successful, rich. Why didn't you grab the nearest horse and gallop to Hollywood after her?"

He sweeps my hair off my shoulder and cups my neck. "Because the woman I want to be with is standing right here in front of me. Looking flat out beautiful. And very, very tempting." He tips his head toward me.

"Tobias, we can't," I murmur.

"You sure about that? Look where you brought me."

Glancing around, I realize I unconsciously led him right to the middle of the Kissing Bridge.

I touch his chest and then my own. "Employee. Employer."

"Not anymore. I quit, remember? About five minutes ago. I'll put it in writing if you want. But, please God, let me kiss you."

My resolve is being flattened, but I try one more time. "You need this job. And the Lazy Dog needs you."

"I'll stay, and I won't touch you again until you hire a new head wrangler. I vote for Amanda. And then I'll wait some more until you hire another wrangler or two. And meanwhile I'll find another job myself, and I'll give you all the equine advice you need the whole time. Satisfied?"

He must see the fear frozen on my face.

"Stop thinking about what might go wrong, Isa." He touches my mouth. "Is this what you want?"

I nod. My body quivers and I'm burning in places that have been iced over for way too long.

"Then we'll figure this out. Ethically. Responsibly. I promise."

His eyes linger on my face until his lips are an inch away. The kiss that comes isn't slow or soft. It isn't tentative, hesitant, searching. It asks and demands. It flames to life like wildfire.

When I pull his body against mine, the fire spreads from my lips to the rest of my body, out of control.

As we come up briefly for air and then melt into each other again, I give up thinking. The Lazy Dog existed before Tobias was head wrangler, and it can exist after him.

Addie and I—with the help of our wacky, lovable crew—can do this. We can hire another wrangler, and I can keep Tobias for myself. Maybe Tyler will let me be a part of his life, too.

I knew what I wanted from the beginning—an amazing wrangler and a successful ranch—and now I have both.

As I kiss Tobias, I can't imagine a better future than a lifetime of him.

Epilogue

Isabel

"Can I take the Zs over to where they're teaching dog tricks?" Tyler asks.

Tobias looks toward where his son points, across the park dotted with people, blankets, pets, and tents, all there for Travis and Amelia's third annual Love & Pets Party. Addie and I promised them we'd be here after their help with Ace last summer, and even with a full house back at the ranch, we managed to sneak away.

"Sure, partner," Tobias says. "But don't take them anywhere else without telling us, okay?"

"I'll go with him." Addie winks at me. "Maybe I'll meet a handsome dog trainer."

"That would be fantastic," I say. "Mine can train the horses, yours can train the dogs."

Tobias' eyes twinkle as he rubs a thumb across the back of my hand he's holding. "Finally."

"What?" Addie asks suspiciously.

"Finally, you two admit those dogs need more training."

Addie swats his arm. I squeeze my hunky cowboy boyfriend's fingers and kiss him, something I've done multiple times every day since he started his new job at a ranch near Lazy Dog.

"Tyler, wait!" Addie hurries after him and the Zs.

"Let's go visit Travis and Amelia," I suggest.

"They aren't hard to find," Tobias says.

We stroll past food trucks, groomers, companies offering yard clean up services, and even a woman claiming to be a cat whisperer, to the bright blue RV parked at the edge of the festival. Travis and Amelia give immunizations and see pets and their owners for free or for a low fee during the event.

A crowd's gathered outside the RV, and I smile when I see what they're looking at. Two adorable pugs play together on the ground.

"Isa, Tobias!" Amelia waves. "So good to see you both. Thank you for coming!"

"Are these the famous Doug and Daisy?" I ask.

When I say his name, the larger pug looks up, his black eyes rolling and tongue flopping out of a black, wrinkly mouth. Daisy takes the opportunity to leap on him and they get back to wrestling in the grass.

Travis hugs me and shakes Tobias' hand. He gestures to a petite brown-haired woman with cat-eye glasses in the group. "Do you remember meeting Beatrix when she came to the ranch?"

Beatrix smiles shyly at me. "I met Travis there for an appointment for my cat, Ever."

"I do remember." Although it was only last July or so, it feels like years ago. I point to the soft-sided cat carrier she holds. "Is that her?"

A black and white cat with pretty green eyes peeks out through the front. "No, this is Fluff. She goes pretty much everywhere with me. Along with this guy." She elbows a compact dark-haired man next to her. "This is my fiancé, Sebastian."

"They're getting married in a few months," Amelia says. "Have you decided where you're going on your honeymoon?"

"Egypt," Sebastian says. "Where cats are held in high regard." He lowers his voice like it's a secret and says to us, "Bea really loves cats."

Travis and Amelia laugh like that's an inside joke. Tobias and I smile at each other. Although we've only been officially dating for about six months, we've already talked about marriage.

He's been working like a, well, like a dog to save up, both to pay for Tyler's past and future medical bills and to buy into the Lazy Dog as a co-owner. Amanda's done a great job since we convinced her to take the head wrangler job, but now that we're at capacity most of the time, Addie and I would love to have Tobias back at the ranch as equine director. He says that even if we're married by then, he won't take the job unless we're on equal financial footing.

Infuriating, exasperating man. But I love him dearly.

And there's Tyler. He and I have been getting along great. Through old Denver friends, I helped score a referral to a renowned pulmonology specialist at Rocky Mountain Hospital for Children in Denver, and he's doing a lot better. Nothing is certain with cystic fibrosis, I've learned, but we'll do everything we can to fight for good care.

"Isa owns a dude ranch," Beatrix tells Sebastian. "We should go! Maybe over summer break when Kate and Will can come with us." To us, she adds, "My eleven-year-old twin niece and nephew would love it."

"You're welcome any time. And Amelia, you and Travis should come up as guests, too. Our treat, after everything you've done for the Zs."

They've made at least three trips to the ranch since last summer, never charging us more than the minimum to cover gas, medicine, and services.

"Dad, Isa, guess what?" Tyler runs over to us leading Zip. Or more like she leads him. "I taught Zip to roll over. And Zap can already shake hands! The trainer gave me treats to keep practicing with them."

He kneels down to show us. Zip focuses on the treat and rolls right over when Tyler tells her to. We all clap, and Tobias introduces his son to the group.

Addie follows behind with Zap and Zoom. The Zs' tails wag furiously when Doug and Daisy greet them. Pugs and weenies together—it's almost too much cuteness in one spot.

Travis steps away from the group to greet a woman with short, curly brown hair walking a slow, stiff, pale-faced Labrador retriever.

"Everyone, this is Sarah Newsome. And this old man is our next patient, Sam." Travis pats the Lab, who peers up at the veterinarian with eyes whitish with age. The dog's tail sways gently. Sarah says hello with a smile, but sadness quickly replaces the pleasant expression. Amelia scoops up Doug and Daisy, Travis lifts Sam into the RV, and Sarah climbs in after them.

"Enjoy the party, everyone. Great to see you!" Amelia says as she closes the door.

Beatrix and Sebastian promise to call for a reservation soon, and we part ways. Addie suggests we grab drinks and find a spot for our blanket.

Feeling completely content, I rest my head on Tobias' strong shoulder as we wait in line behind Addie, Tyler, and the Zs at a food truck. My wonderful twenty-legged tribe.

The future will hold challenges, I'm sure, but we're ready to meet them. All together.

THE END

A.G. HENLEY

It all started with a girl, a boy, and a pug named Doug.
Get the exclusive Love & Pets prequel for FREE!

Love & Pets Book 4:
Can he help mend her dogeared heart?
Read The Lessons of Labradors now!

Read Next

The Lessons of Labradors: Love & Pets #4

Chapter One
Sarah

Lost Paws, Session One

I take a seat in the circle of chairs in the basement meeting room of Most Glorious Blood of Christ Catholic Church and watch nervously as other group members make their way in. I'm clutching the framed picture of Sam that I'd spent an embar-rassing amount of time selecting.

A few faded religious posters hang on the walls of the sparsely furnished room, and thin industrial carpet lines the floor. A whiteboard is at the head of the circle next to an empty chair. The room looks like . . . the basement meeting room of any one of thousands of churches around the United States.

I wasn't sure what to expect when I signed up for a pet grief support group, and to be honest, I'm still not sure I made the right decision to come.

It's Tuesday night, one of my few evenings off from the library, and I have a lot of adulting to do. But as my best friend Angela told me, if I don't climb back onto the train of life, it's going to pass me by . . . and royally screw up my hair as it goes. I take a deep breath. I can do this.

A middle-aged woman with dark blonde hair swept up in a pile on her head comes my way wearing an empathic smile. Although it's the last day of March in Colorado—which means it's flipping freezing—she's wearing capri pants, hiking-style sandals with socks, and a white T-shirt featuring a screen-printed photograph of an equally blonde cocker spaniel. The resem-blance between the dog and the T-shirt wearer is seriously uncanny.

The woman greets me, her voice warm. "I'm Bev Philson, the leader of the Lost Paws group. May I see your fur baby?"

With a small smile, I hold out the picture of Sam for her.

"Oh, a yellow Labrador retriever!" she says. "What wonder-ful, loyal dogs they are. You must be . . . Sarah Newsome?"

Wow, Bev read my sign-up form thoroughly. I nod and stand to shake her outstretched hand. She grabs mine with both of hers and pumps it up and down.

"So nice to meet you. Thank you for joining the group. We'll get started in a few minutes."

I settle myself back in my chair, swiping at the chocolate

curls that fall in my eyes whenever I move my head, as Bev greets the woman in the plain metal chair next to me.

My neighbor has salt-and-pepper hair pulled back in a low bun, she wears all black from head to toe, a large silver cross hangs at her neck, and a framed image of a massive Saint Bernard rests on her knees. The dog looks friendly in a slobbery sort of way. The older woman smells like baby powder, which reminds me of my grandmother back in Omaha.

Bev greets her and oohs and aahs over the dog before moving on to the twenty-something man slouching in a chair across the circle, no pet picture in sight. His jeans are full of holes, and his metal band sweatshirt has paint stains on it. I think he was staring at my boobs a minute ago.

Next to him, an African American woman talks with an older Latino man. They have pictures, too. I'm relieved to see I'm not the only fool clutching a picture of my dead dog.

I'm preparing to eavesdrop on Bev's conversation with the others when I catch sight of a new guy walking in. My mouth drops open, and my breath catches.

He wears jeans, a pale-green button-down shirt, and loafers. His brown hair is shorter than it used to be, and although he's too far away to see this, his eyes are a gorgeous shade of spring green and fall gold.

I know that because I'd stared at them often enough back in college when he would come into the library where I'd worked part-time.

Ben Becker. It's been six years since I've seen him, but he still looks good enough to eat with whipped cream and sprinkles. My heart, cold and still for the last six months, unexpectedly pumps. Probably feeling me staring at him like a cat that found a bird lunching on its scratching post, Ben glances at me.

I look away. I won't give him the satisfaction of showing him I remember him. Not after the way we'd ended things. I turn instead to Bev, who sits in the empty chair at the front after briefly greeting Ben. She beams at each of us in turn.

"Good evening, everyone, and welcome to our first session! This is Lost Paws, the pet grief support group. If you're here for Celibrate—the support group that celebrates celibacy—it's on Saturday nights at nine o'clock. An excellent day and time for it, don't you think?"

She stops, waiting for us to laugh. I smile uncomfortably and avoid looking anywhere near Ben. Which isn't easy—he's sitting across from me, next to the slouchy guy.

Bev composes her face and her tone takes a serious turn. "We're all here because we've lost someone close to us."

My gut clenches. I will *not* cry in the first minute of the group session. The older woman beside me digs in her purse and pulls out a tissue. I pat her back, and she offers me a watery smile. At least I won't be the first one to leak.

"That includes me." Bev pulls her shirt out from her chest so we can see the cocker spaniel better. "This is Adorabelle—Belle —my fur baby who crossed over the Rainbow Bridge nearly ten years ago now."

No. Please. Not the Rainbow Bridge again. Sam's waiting for me there, or so my neighbor and good friend Rose Bush tells me. And yes, that's her actual name.

I prefer to think of Sam lounging on a couch made of clouds, lunching on as many Vienna sausages as he can before ambling down a wide mountain path with tons of chipmunks to chase. Now that would be his idea of heaven, not some bridge made of water and light.

"My own struggle to heal my broken heart after Belle's death is what led me to start Lost Paws," Bev says. "I'm a licensed professional counselor, trained right here in Fort Collins. I completed my graduate degree through Colorado State University's Department of Psychology."

I have an even harder time not sneaking a peek at Ben. CSU is our alma mater, too.

"I have a private practice focusing on helping older folks with food fetishes," Bev says, "but I save one night a week for this group. It holds a special place in my heart."

The African American woman and I exchange an *um, okay* look. Talk about a niche.

Bev picks up a piece of paper from her chair. "Now, before we get to know each other better, I'd like to lay out the ground rules for the group. First, like in Las Vegas, what happens in the group stays in the group. That's everything from information as basic as our names to things shared in session." She gives us a stern look. "Confidentiality is essential to any therapeutic endeavor.

"Second, please try to be on time and attend all sessions. Healing only happens if you're here, friends." She beams at us.

"Third, no talking about group members when they aren't in group. No one likes to be talked about behind their back, do they? And fourth, no socializing outside of group. Friendly interactions before or after group is acceptable, of course, but friendships should wait at least until group concludes on May nineteenth." I again avoid Ben's eyes as Bev pauses. "Any questions?"

The sloucher raises his hand. "Has anyone, like, hooked up with someone in the group before?" He glances at me and cocks an eyebrow.

I wince. Please tell me the first man under sixty to be interested in me in months is not the one who looks like he rolled out of the Narcotics Anonymous group that's probably here on Monday nights to confess their weekend sins. The patrons of the library skew towards elderly, and I've had my fair share of being hit on by baby boomers with too much Viagra on their hands.

"I'm sure it's happened," Bev says, "but not until after the group ended." She claps her hands. "Okay, I know it can be a little stressful to speak in front of a group of strangers, so we'll do an icebreaking exercise with a partner first." She holds up three fingers and wiggles them around. Gold rings wink from several digits. "I'd like you and your partner to share three things about yourself: your name, your pet's name, and the thing you miss the most about them."

Crap. I'm going to cry for sure. But it's time to tear the Band-Aid off, I guess. I turn to the woman next to me as Bev adds, "Why don't you pair up with the person sitting directly across from you?"

The sloucher across the circle grins like he's won a free year of Playboy TV, while the smile I was in the process of painting on starts to drip. It gets worse when Ben jumps up and heads my way with a smile and a raised eyebrow.

"Hey, partner."

Okay, he *could* have been my knight in organic cotton and selvage denim. Except that, six years ago, he lied and broke my heart.

The panic sets in again. I'm partnering with Ben Becker, my gorgeous ex-boyfriend—if you can call someone you only went out with a handful times that—while blubbering uncontrollably about Sam.

On second thought, give me the slouch.

Read The Lessons of Labradors: Love & Pets #4

Acknowledgments

I have several people to thank for helping me get this book written and ready to publish, but first I want to share a few notes.

The Downside of Dachshunds was inspired by two things from my own life. First, a summer spent working at the glorious C Lazy U Ranch in Colorado while I was in college. I was a housekeeper, and I learned several things from my job:

- Housekeepers are underpaid and under-appreciated
- People are *really* messy
- The wait staff got all the perks (tips, relationships with guests, etc.)

There was no Cliff (or, sadly, Tobias). But I was able to ride horses, mountain bike, and make great friends from around the United States, surrounded by a beautiful Rocky Mountain setting.

Just after I went back to school, Cindy Crawford and Richard Gere visited. Talk about lousy timing. At least I got to write my own celebrity visit into the book.

The Zs were inspired by my own sweet dachshund mix,

Zippy. She lived to be fifteen, and by the end of her life she had a bad back and only one eye, but she never stopped loving us. What a great dog she was. Thank you to my daughter Arden for the Zs' names. I asked what I should call them and lickety-split, she had them.

Many, many thanks go to my beta readers, Lorie Humpherys, Kathy Azzolina, Sandy Grant, and Saundra Wright who poured over the book finding spelling, grammatical, and other mistakes, of which there were many. I'm so grateful that they're willing to spend their time helping me in this way. Any remaining errors are mine.

I also appreciate my cover designer, Najla Qamber, who is talented, professional, and quick. Thank you to my ARC Team members who review my books, and my readers in general. I love hearing from you and I'm so glad you're with me. Thank you so much!

Finally and always, my family. As I write this the week before Thanksgiving 2019, I'm most grateful for you. Love to you all.

Also by A. G. Henley

The Love & Pets Series (Sweet Romantic Comedy)

Love, Pugs, and Other Problems: A Love & Pets Prequel Story

The Problem with Pugs

The Trouble with Tabbies

The Downside of Dachshunds

The Lessons of Labradors

The Predicament of Persians

The Conundrum of Collies

The Pandemonium of Pets: A Love & Pets Christmas Romance

The Love & Pets Series Box Set: Books 1 - 3

Nicole Rossi Thrillers (Young Adult)

Double Black Diamond

The Brilliant Darkness Series (Young Adult Fantasy)

The Scourge

The Keeper: A Brilliant Darkness Story

The Defiance

The Gatherer: A Brilliant Darkness Story

The Fire Sisters

The Brilliant Darkness Boxed Set

Novellas (Young Adult Fantasy)

Untimely

Featured in *Tick Tock: Seven Tales of Time*

Basil and Jade

Featured in *Off Beat: Nine Spins on Song*

The Escape Room

Featured in *Dead Night: Four Fits of Fear*

About the Author

A.G. Henley is a *USA Today* bestselling author of novels and stories in multiple genres including thrillers, romantic comedies, and fantasy romances. The first book in her young adult Brilliant Darkness series, *The Scourge*, was a Library Journal Self-e Selection and a Next Generation Indie Book Award finalist. She's also a clinical psychologist, but she promises not to analyze you . . . much.

Find her at:
aghenley.com
Email Aimee

CPSIA information can be obtained
at www.ICGtesting.com
Printed in the USA
LVHW021658070621
689582LV00006B/1162

9 780999 655252